GREEK GOD
Navy SEALs of Valor 4

SABRINA DEVONSHIRE

To Tina,
   Best wishes,

[signature]

This work is copyright. No part may be reproduced, copied, scanned, stored in a retrieval system, recorded or transmitted in any form, or by any means without the prior written permission of the author except by reviewers who may use brief excerpts as part of a review.

Please purchase only authorized editions, and do not participate in or encourage piracy of copyrighted materials. Your support of the author's rights is appreciated.

This book is a work of fiction. Names, characters, places, and incidents either are products of the author's imagination or are used fictitiously. Any resemblance to actual events or locales or persons, living or dead, is entirely coincidental.

Greek God (Navy Seals of Valor 4)
Copyright © 2015 Sabrina Devonshire
ISBN: 978-1518621833
Published by Corazon del Oro
Communications, LLC
Cover art by Anya Kelleye

ACKNOWLEDGMENTS

I wish to thank Marion Cook for her diligent editing work and Patricia Dawson and Christopher Ferko for their excellent copyediting support.

PREFACE

May 24, 2016
Athens International Airport
0900 hours

An evil smile crept over Farid's face. He felt light-headed, almost delirious with excitement. It was an honor to be one of Allah's chosen people, placed on Earth to establish a pure race of Muslims and to cleanse the world of the lesser beings. A thrill rushed through his veins every time he violently ended the life of an infidel. *The time to rage war on the Americans has come.* His heart beat faster as he imagined brutally slaying the men who had interfered with his purposeful mission of Jihad.

The three American Navy SEALs he'd been waiting for deplaned from their Dulles-to-Athens flight, two of them with women on their arms.

Nathan Brooks — resigned from the Navy in February of 2015 before being hired by the U.S. Department of State. Travels under dozens of different identities. The woman hanging on his arm is former Air Force Captain Baylee Stiles.

He'd managed to tail Brooks after a recent extraction mission in Syria. Eavesdropping on two of the bastard's cell phone conversations gleaned him information about his plans to travel to Greece for a wedding.

He narrowed his eyes at the SEAL with the reddish-brown hair who walked with attitude as well as athletic grace, one arm slung around the shoulders of a very attractive brunette. *Darryl Jennings — Petty Officer First Class with DEVGRU. He managed to keep his identity a secret until one of our IT analysts hacked into the flight list. Clinging to his arm is his fiancé and CIA agent, Olivia Simpson.*

A third SEAL, nearly as muscle bound as Brooks, strode behind the other two men wearing a serious expression on his face. *Karl Patterson — Petty Officer First Class. A man of few words. Appears to be highly intelligent. But not smart enough to know I'm studying every move he makes.*

The three sailors had made a major tactical error traveling on a commercial flight. But they'd apparently wanted to travel like every day civilians to show their female companions a good time. *Think they're safe, do they? How wrong they are.* Farid burst out into maniacal laughter, inciting uneasy stares from passengers walking past him. The fear he saw in their eyes gave him a jolt of pleasure.

Brooks and his other American SEAL, Delta, and Green Beret compatriots had delivered several lethal blows to Muslim Alliance terror operations. The fear their organization had instilled in the American public had begun to subside. *Once we make an example out of these men, every U.S. citizen will suffer from night terrors.* Farid cackled out loud, covering his mouth to muffle his laughter.

The travelers in the Athens airport would be permitted to board their tour buses so they could go to the Parthenon and the Temple of Zeus and buy trinkets from shops along the steep narrow streets. No death would come to them today. The three SEALs would be safe for now. Only later would they suffer the consequences for what they'd done. *I could gun them all down at this moment if I wanted to.* The fake flight attendant badge he'd obtained with a hefty bribe kept him clear of the X-ray machines. *But that would ruin all the fun.*

A sudden death for Brooks, Jennings and Patterson would be too quick and comfortable. He wanted to watch them suffer. He would insert the knife in the gut and metaphorically twist it over and over again by torturing and killing their women.

The analytical and quiet Patterson seemed to be a lone ranger, but Jennings and Brooks were — what was that American term so often used? Oh, yes, pussy whipped. As they walked toward baggage claim, Jennings clung to his wife-to-be, Olivia Simpson. Brooks and his girlfriend, Baylee Stiles, locked lips so often, they stumbled more than walked. *I'm sure they'll fuck each other's brains out the minute they get to their hotel.*

Of the two women, Stiles irritated him the most. He wasn't sure if it was her shrill voice or her assertive, unfeminine mannerisms. Her almost white blond hair and the scattered freckles on her face made her look fragile and dainty, like a woman should be. But her true personality was that of a bold aggressor, a no-good slut. He'd initially planned to snatch Olivia, but listening to Baylee's raucous laughter was enough to change his mind. He narrowed his eyes at the fair-headed woman and every muscle in his body twitched with hatred.

Get ready to die, bitch.

CHAPTER ONE

May 25, 2016
Nikiana Hotel
Lefkada Island, Greece
1330 hours

Jamie Phillips stood in front of the painted tile countertop in the Nikiana Hotel lobby. Her ankles crossed, she tucked an unruly lock of hair behind her ear and fidgeted with her passport while she waited for her room key.

She stared at the desk attendant's back as she reached into a wooden cubby to pick up a key. It was better to notice the dress's watermelon color and the way the slightly bunched up straps dipped into a u-shape instead of allowing her gaze to wander back to the window. *So what if the hotel is perched high on a cliff and overlooks the Ionian Sea. So what if the water is such a rich, deep sapphire, it looks too postcard beautiful to be real. So what if people say the water's cool, refreshing, and crystal clear and jumping in would probably make me instantly feel more alive. I won't look out that window again. I won't rush out to take a dip in the sea. I won't allow myself to fall for this place.* Immersing her senses in the romance of the Greek Islands would only intensify her longing.

The front door opened, ushering in a hot arid breeze and the aroma of jasmine and roses. Jamie defiantly breathed through her mouth. She wouldn't inhale a nose full of that fragrant, sweet scent that brought back memories of Luxembourg Park and Paris in springtime. She wouldn't let her thoughts linger on the love affair that had blossomed there.

She vowed not to be moved one iota by the colorful hand-painted tiles that made the floor under her feet look like a work of art or the tall decorative palms spilling out of enormous glazed pots that set an exotic, tropical vacation mood.

This Greek island wasn't an idyllic piece of paradise. It was a metal-barred prison holding her hostage to old feelings better forgotten. She longed to curl up on her well-worn couch in her Paris apartment to watch a spy movie or read a book, to hole up in a place she felt safe rather than vulnerable and out-of-sorts.

Darryl and Olivia's wedding had brought her to Greece. In three days, they would exchange vows barefoot on a nearby beach. She found it hard to imagine the serious-minded Navy SEAL removing his shoes. She'd imagined him standing on the stage in his dress uniform with an erect posture and freshly shined shoes.

She'd met Darryl Jennings in Charles de Gaulle airport in the middle of a crisis. He hadn't shown a single sign of losing his cool even after chemical weapons were deployed and his team took heavy fire.

She'd seen one wry smile quirk the corner of Darryl's lips when he'd told his men they could prolong their Paris stay to "wrap up paperwork." That mischievous smile had everything to do with Darryl noticing the attraction brewing between Jamie and Karl. During those few days the SEALs had lingered in Paris, she'd gotten to know Darryl, Nathan, and Baylee over French food and wine.

Like her and Karl, Darryl was an avid football fan. They'd joked and laughed, able to recite scores from every pro football game the previous season. The week had been like an amazing dream. She'd fallen so in love with Karl her feet barely touched the ground as she walked. And she'd felt so comfortable and accepted by his circle of friends. *If only it could have worked out.*

She whispered Karl's name under her breath as a rush of nostalgia washed over her. *Our love affair was such a crazy, out-of-control whirlwind.* Her nerve endings tingled as if an electric current ran through her bloodstream. Her nipples hardened as an image of her former lover naked flashed in front of her face. *Sweat glistening on the contours of his wide jaw, the firm ridges of his chest, and on his tight muscular thighs.* Her pulse raced as she recalled the sensual pleasures they'd shared.

It was inevitable she'd run into him any minute. Karl and Darryl were fast friends as well as members of the same SEAL team. *It's going to be awkward if I don't get a grip.*

Her passport stuck to her sweaty hands. *I just arrived and already I'm a wreck. Stop thinking about him.*

Tingles raced across her skin while her muscles tensed. She hadn't seen him since last July. *What will it be like seeing him again?*

It will be terrible, she thought before another jolt of sexual excitement raced through her veins. *I shouldn't want to see him. Especially now. I look like complete hell.* After flying from Paris to Athens, she'd boarded a bus. The five-hour journey took the passengers across the mainland, over the immense Rio-Antirrio suspension bridge spanning the Gulf of Corinth and then over a rugged, mountainous section of the Peloponnese peninsula before traversing the marshlands that led to Lefkada Island.

Wind from open windows had blown her hair into a mass of tangles. She drummed her fingers on the countertop. The attendant now held the key in her hand, but was looking through a file. *Is it possible for her to move any slower?*

She had become accustomed to long waits and slower moving people since she'd moved to France. A frenetic pace wasn't common in most countries the way it was in America. But today, her patience had flown. All she cared about now was getting from the lobby to her room without being seen. *With any luck, I still will.*

Not that it had been a jackpot day. Her luggage had been lost by the airlines, the bus had departed an hour late, the air-conditioning on the bus hadn't been working and she'd unwisely seated herself beside a woman with garlic breath who barely stopped talking to breathe.

Jamie's posture sagged under the weight of her frustration. Irate moods weren't the norm for her. Now everything seemed to annoy her. *Why didn't I just mail Darryl and Olivia a wedding gift and politely say I'm sorry, I can't make it?* She'd never even met his bride to be. She blocked out the voice in her head that said *you're here to see Karl again.* Their end had happened so suddenly she sometimes wondered if it had been a mistake. *No. It's over between us. Seeing him again will only complicate things.*

She'd walked straight into the fire by coming to Greece and would pay dearly for it. A surge of anxiety threatened to burst from her chest. She wrung her hands and tugged on the cotton fabric of her sundress that clung to her sweaty thighs. *Why do relationships have to be so complicated? Just when you think you know what you want, you realize you have no clue.*

She struggled to redirect her thoughts. *I need to focus on getting my hands on an appropriate dress.* The one she'd planned to wear to the wedding was neatly packed in the suitcase that had been tagged in Paris, but hadn't made it to the luggage carousel in Athens. Who knew where it was now — Athens, Georgia, perhaps?

Maybe the attendant can recommend a shop in town. She pictured herself wearing a white cotton dress similar to ones the chic Greek women wore in the fashion magazine she'd flipped through in an Athens airport shop. It could be fun picking out a body-hugging dress with stylish cutouts and stitched accents along the neckline and hem. *He'd notice me for sure in that.*

Her patience with her unwieldy thoughts was running out. *You have to stop thinking about him. Now.*

"Here you go, ma'am. Enjoy your stay." The dark-haired woman slid a key across the desk. Her row of sturdy straight teeth looked snow white against her tanned skin.

In addition to buying a dress, some time for sunning her skin to a more attractive pallor would need to be built into the itinerary.

"Thank you." Jamie debated about asking the attendant for suggestions on local clothing shops. After settling in her room, she could run out and shop before she got too comfortable and collapsed for the night. "I have a qu—" Her words caught in her throat the instant she heard that familiar deep, southern-accented voice.

Warm heat climbed up her neck, sending tremors of excitement scattering through her body. *Damn.* She'd forgotten how overpowering his nearness felt. *So intoxicating.* Even with her back to him, she imagined looking into those ocean blue eyes that had stolen every ounce of air from her lungs when he'd scooped her up in his arms and rushed her out of the burning hotel in Paris. *I can't take this.*

Wrenching her mouth into a smile, she whirled around to face him. Her neck and shoulder muscles tensed. What first struck her was how drool worthy he looked. Blue jeans hugged his sturdy, muscular thighs and a black polo shirt stretched across the strong breadth of his chest making his shoulders look broader than ever. His dark hair, once trimmed close to the scalp, had grown longer and looked messy and windblown. Next, she made the irritating observation that he was speaking to an athletic and extremely attractive woman. *Obviously, he's forgotten about me.*

She counted the tiles separating them to regain her composure. *Eight, nine, ten.* His magnetism was so potent, he felt far less distant. A whiff of his woodsy, masculine scent drifted into her nostrils.

She closed her eyes, unable to stop herself from breathing him in. That mingling of pine and cinnamon and manly sweat brought back so many memories. Memories of the nights they'd made love until dawn, the leisurely strolls they'd taken while holding hands and intermittently kissing in Luxembourg Park, and the conversations they'd had about their future.

Then genius me ruined it all with one call. The weight of their end had left a permanent empty ache inside her chest. Sometimes she found herself inadvertently placing a hand over that spot as if to alleviate that hollow pain.

What else could I have done? Things weren't working out once our lives went back to normal. I accepted permanent work with France 24 and Karl dropped off the radar for months sometimes. Suggesting we date other people made sense.

The lovely brunette with Karl tossed her head back and laughed. Her thick dark hair bounced like it would if she were being filmed for a shampoo ad. Jamie wondered if the pain jabbing into her stomach would feel less intense if the woman had pockmarks on her face.

This woman's graceful beauty fit Jamie's vision of what a man as startlingly handsome as Karl would want. *Beautiful in a no-nonsense kind of way.* The woman didn't even have to try to look good. Her short cropped hair turned under neatly just below her ears. Her lack of makeup did nothing to detract from her looks. Her soft, smooth complexion glowed with apparent health. Her hand brushed against his forearm and he made no move to pull away.

Jamie's fingers unfurled from her clenched fists. It was as if she were instinctively reaching, imagining the pads of her fingers landing on the surface of Karl's warm, masculine skin. She imagined the sigh of satisfaction she would feel ending this torture of so many months apart with one touch.

He wants to touch her now, not you. Jamie's hands trembled with jealousy. Anger at her childish reaction mingled with the surge of frustration over seeing another woman's hands on him. *I have no right to be jealous. He's not mine now. Maybe he never was.*

She wanted to cover her face and cry. Scream. Run as far from this unfamiliar hotel lobby as she could. *Oh, no. I have to get out of here.* "Excuse me, Miss. You had a question for me?" The front desk attendant gazed at her with curious brown eyes.

Jamie was so flustered she couldn't remember what she'd planned to ask. "Uh, don't worry, it wasn't important." She took a shaky step back from the desk before tucking her passport into the outside pocket of her small backpack.

"Wait, Miss, your key."

"Oh, yes, of course." Her voice sounded panicked. The thread of composure she'd managed to maintain was about to break. Jamie pivoted back toward the desk and lunged for the key. Once she snatched it from the counter, she glanced in Karl's direction with a bowed head, desperately hoping he wouldn't see her.

He's far too occupied with Miss Naturally Beautiful. Why would he notice the ex-girlfriend with the tangled hair and faded sundress?

Jamie clenched her teeth as she watched him lean in to embrace the woman. *Oh, God, he's hugging her. And she doesn't have an ounce of fat on her body. I look like a ripe blueberry in this dress next to her. That's it. I'm out of here.*

As she jerked her body into motion, one of her sandals slid on the smooth, slick tile, slightly wet from people passing through from the pool. One leg lurched out in front until she was dangerously close to doing the splits. She jerked her legs back together and walked faster all the time telling herself she shouldn't be jealous, that it was over, that she shouldn't still be pining for him after all this time. But her brain refused to cooperate. Her will had lost the battle against her heart.

At least he didn't see me. I'll do a fierce karate workout until I feel like my in-control self again. She'd tame her traitorous heart by exhausting her body. Then she wouldn't have any energy left to feel.

"Jamie, is that you?"

Oh, no. That familiar southern accent and the deep masculine tenor of his voice set every nerve ending on high alert. Her heart beat so fast and loud she heard what sounded like a frenetic drumbeat inside her ears. *What should I do now?*

She jerked to a halt, debating on whether to stop or run. *I can't face him now. Not like this.* With her back still turned to him, she made her decision. Without saying a word, she walked toward the stairwell.

CHAPTER TWO

May 25, 2016
Nikiana Hotel
Lefkada Island, Greece
1340 hours

Karl's heart rate accelerated the instant he noticed her. He'd expected to feel a tinge of pain when he saw Jamie again, but not to be bowled over like this. The tangle of strawberry-blond hair falling over her bare shoulders reminded him of how she'd looked on mornings when they'd awakened in bed together after a long night of crazy, passionate sex. And the way her blue sundress clung to her buttocks and thighs conjured up images of her voluptuous body naked and how he'd possessed it in a variety of hedonistic ways. Seeing the stricken expression on her face had physically hurt. He felt as if someone had punched a fist through his abdominal muscles, gripped his intestines and twisted them into knots.

For months, he'd clung to the possibility of reconciliation. He'd found himself fantasizing about it during the days leading up to the trip. Now, he realized just how unrealistic his thoughts had been. Their relationship was so over for her, she couldn't even stomach some strained pleasantries. Karl huffed out a frustrated sigh.

Long-term relationships were outside the realm of his comfort zone. Once he'd met Jamie, his predictable black and white world had splintered into agonizing shades of gray. He longed for the safety of structured planning, mathematical equations and logic. A methodological approach to life had served him well for so many years. Now he had to cope with this unwelcome bombardment of emotions.

Why can't she at least say hello? Don't obsess. Let her go, his logical mind suggested. *Chasing her will only escalate the drama.* Drama he wasn't used to coping with.

As she walked away, he felt like she was dragging bits of his heart along with her. He shook his head and sighed. *Why am I still so caught up in this? In her?*

Before he could clamp his lips shut, he shouted, "Jamie, wait." His voice echoed through the high-ceilinged room. As the door leading outside slammed behind her, he let his hands drop to his thighs and shook his head.

"That went well." Olivia studied him with a puzzled expression. "What's up with that?"

Karl gave Darryl's bride-to-be a wry smile. "The way she stormed out of here, you'd think I dumped her, wouldn't you? She was the one who suggested we start dating other people." The painful wrenching inside his chest hurt every bit as much now as it had the moment he'd learned he'd lost the woman he loved. *That I still love, damn it.*

Olivia's eyes widened and looked at him with what looked too much like pity. "Oh, that's what happened."

"Yep. Even worse, she delivered the blow on the phone." Karl had been so battered by the incident he hadn't spoken about it to anyone, not even his closest friends Nathan and Darryl. They must have imagined their relationship had been headed toward marriage once he had mentioned plans to change careers instead of re-upping when his enlistment contract ended in December. Until recently, nothing except DEVGRU business occupied his mind. Just when he'd come to believe there was more to life than the next mission, his relationship with Jamie had slipped away in less than a minute.

"Damn, Karl. That had to have hurt. But I'm wondering..." Jutting one hip out, she paused for a moment and tapped a finger on the side of her face. "Maybe there's more to this than meets the eye. Jamie looked ready to burst into tears and her hands were shaking. I think she scurried off because she didn't want you to see how upset she was. And you know...after a breakup, a person can conjure up all sorts of dreadful scenarios. She probably saw us talking and thought I was your new girlfriend."

Karl frowned. "No way. Are you serious?"

"Yes, I'm serious. If I had been in her shoes, I would have been jealous, too."

"Really. Why? She dumped me, remember."

Olivia's voice sounded slightly impatient. "Yes, but you don't really know why. What we do know is she was upset and felt too vulnerable to face you. Wait until she's calmed down and then try again. She'll talk to you, I'm sure of it."

Karl released a long, frustrated sigh. "I should just let her get on with her life. She had a good reason to call off our relationship. It was great at first, but all the time we spent apart changed things. She lives a busy life as a broadcast journalist and you know what it's like to live with a DEVGRU guy."

"Did she complain about you being gone so much?"

He sighed. "No, not once." A sad heaviness settled in his chest. Compared to other women he'd dated, Jamie had been surprisingly low maintenance. There'd been no complaining, no whining, no tears. He'd never had to duck to avoid being struck by a flung plate or to shield his ears from a screaming outburst. Jamie had never lashed out at him.

She had an outspoken streak for sure, but for the most part she was all smiles and laughter. The last time he'd seen her, she'd been unusually quiet and pensive. She must have needed something from the relationship that he hadn't provided. *If only she had spoken up, I would have tried harder to make her happy.* He wanted to give her everything.

"So you think she called it off because you were drifting apart?"

"Yes. Once it was clear to her things were heading south, she must have made her decision. I should have acted sooner to try to turn things around, but I'm not exactly a relationship expert."

The more he'd missed Jamie, the more he'd lost his edge. His signature focus had begun to slip. After a couple of minor, but noticeable tactical errors he'd made on a mission, Master Chief Drake had called him into his office and read him the riot act. Pissing off Drake was never a good idea. But instead of reassuring the Chief it would never happen again, which would have been his normal modus operandi, he'd sat there in stony silence resenting the long weeks away that no longer felt worth the sacrifice.

It wasn't that protecting his country no longer mattered or that he wasn't committed to supporting his DEVGRU team. After twelve years of committed service he had reached a juncture where he needed more dimension to his life than sweaty training sessions and dangerous missions.

Whenever he returned stateside to Alabama, his Huntsville apartment seemed to mock him, saying, *what kind of home is this?* He wanted a real house, real furniture and a family.

He wanted a sturdy brick home with large windows and black shutters with an acre of lush green grass behind it where a dog could bound around and chase a ball while his children played soccer or freeze tag.

He wanted a house filled with comfortable furniture instead of the lumpy sofa with stuffing pushing out from the worn fabric. Before Jamie, that had been the only piece of furniture he'd owned other than a mattress and box springs, a plastic table and chairs and a tattered bookshelf he'd bought at a garage sale.

For years, he hadn't felt in any way deprived living in his bare essentials apartment.

Only when Jamie stepped inside for the first time and he watched her mouth fall open in dismay and shock did he realize his living quarters were a disgrace. She hadn't masked her shock. In fact, she'd burst out with, "Holy crap. This place looks like a guys dorm room. All that's missing is the trashcan overflowing with empty beer cans."

He'd jumped to defend his man cave where he spent hours snoozing, drinking beer and watching ball games whenever he was on leave. He was a Navy SEAL, not an interior decorator. He was trained to kill and execute missions not to know which colors blended well or what kind of furniture suited a room.

Once his bruised ego had rebounded, he had walked through his apartment and tried to see it through Jamie's eyes. Yes, the poster of the New England Patriots pinned to the wall looked terribly tacky with its dog-eared corners and off-center placement. His enormous flat screen TV was indeed awesome, but would probably look neater seated on a table instead of a stack of cement blocks.

He'd asked Jamie for suggestions and she had waved her hands around and bounced up on her toes, full of ideas on what could be done. The next day, they had strolled hand-in-hand through a furniture store. They spent the day plopping down on beds, chairs and couches and talking about what might look good in each of the rooms.

A week later, the living room and bedroom suite they had picked out had been delivered. He'd placed a hold on a kitchen table and chairs to be processed after two more pay periods.

One morning Jamie had walked through the door her arms overloaded with framed photographs of picturesque scenes she'd purchased at a garage sale.

He'd laughed in delight when she pulled out a New England Patriots banner that she'd had framed for him from a separate bag. After they'd talked about placement and hung all the wares on the walls, Karl had felt surprisingly content with the embellishments.

Not only did his apartment feel more comfortable and homey, having Jamie's lively presence in the apartment felt so right. Just hearing the sound of her rinsing a dish in the kitchen or opening a cupboard made him feel like she belonged to him and was an intimate part of his life.

Subsequent visits had been equally memorable; full of late night chats, long walks and lovemaking, until one particular day. He wasn't sure whether it had been too much time apart or whether both of them had changed, but when he'd arrived on Jamie's doorstep and she'd opened the door, they'd both paused for a moment, studying each other before moving into an embrace. During that long moment, he'd seen the beauty of her curvy physique and the way her reddish blond hair framed her face, but there was hardness in her expression, a lack of sparkle in her blue green eyes. He felt as if he were admiring an attractive stranger, not a woman who was his. Had she felt that shift as well?

Throughout the visit, the broken connection seemed to become increasingly evident. Long, awkward periods of silence occupied time that had once been filled with cozy conversation. Then they'd both speak at once and apologize. And after a short burst of forced conversation, silence would stretch out into what felt like infinity.

The last time Jamie had visited, Karl had been miserable. Even their lovemaking had felt mechanical and contrived. Their relationship was in its death throes and he had known the only way to resuscitate it was for them to spend more time together. That would mean risking everything on the hope that the intimate bond they'd once shared were recoverable.

After investigating employment opportunities with the U.S. Department of State, Karl spent months planning how he'd transition to this new line of work once his Navy contract ended. When he'd had an unexpected opportunity in Kabul to make personal calls, excitement had surged through his veins as he'd dialed Jamie's number, planning to share his well thought out plan. Before he'd had a chance to mention it, she'd stunned him with her dating other people suggestion.

He'd dropped the phone onto the dusty ground, fumbled for it and forced himself to say, "Yeah, we can do that," instead of pleading with her the way he'd wanted to.

He would have sounded like an idiot telling her about the long satellite phone conversations he'd had with Nathan or sharing his well-calculated plan that could have ended their long days and nights of separation. *Fuck.*

"You two need to talk," said Olivia. "It's obvious this break up isn't working for either one of you."

Karl wiped sweat from his brow and sighed. Even though Jamie's actions suggested she despised him, her hurt expression suggested she was suffering. He couldn't stand the thought of being responsible for her pain.

Why do women say one thing and mean another? That had to be the question of the century. Women were damn complicated, but they also had amazing perspective when it came to reading people's feelings. Olivia's comments were a clear example of that. Pain jabbed into his gut as he recalled how his beloved sister Kelsi had always sensed whenever he needed a listening ear.

How had she known that if he gobbled down two bowls of cereal after school in less than five minutes it meant he'd had a horrible day? Each time he'd dropped the empty bowl in the sink and retreated to his room, a soft knock at his door had followed.

After he'd told his sister she could come in, she'd open the door, stride over and plop down on his bed. She'd say something right on target, like, "I guess that physics test didn't go too well" or "I take it Amanda said no to the prom idea."

Karl could never look at someone's expression or watch a person eat and conclude what might be going on in his or her head. His three brothers were every bit as oblivious to analyzing feelings as Karl. But damn it if Kelsi couldn't read his distress every time. She'd always been there whenever he'd needed support growing up.

Fifteen years had passed since her death in the terrorist-struck North Tower, yet the hollow ache of her absence had never subsided. He knew it never would. He'd always been close to his parents and other siblings and valued time spent stateside with them, but he'd loved his sister the most.

When his relationship with Jamie had been at it's apex, he'd imagined making her a part of their close-knit family unit. Suddenly, that plan had disintegrated into a lost dream. For the first time in a long time, a flicker of hope surfaced. If Olivia's intuitions were correct, perhaps the relationship could still be salvaged.

"All right. I'll take another shot at talking to her and just hope she doesn't run away this time."

"Don't worry. I have an idea," said Olivia. Her eyes twinkled with mischief.

If Darryl's soon-to-be-wife had an idea up her sleeve, it was sure to be a good one.

CHAPTER THREE

May 25, 2016
Nikiana Hotel
Lefkada Island, Greece
1345 hours

Jamie race walked down the stone path that led to her complex of milk-white, three tier apartments. After taking the stairs to the second level two at a time and entering her room, she sagged against the closed door, her breaths short and raspy. That nagging voice in her head saying *ending your relationship was a mistake* escalated to a scream. *Damn it. Why am I freaking out?* I did the right thing. Karl had been out-of-touch on missions for weeks or months at a time. And ever since she had earned a permanent position as a broadcast journalist with France 24, she'd worked after hours most days partly because she loved digging up lead stories and partly to hide from the loneliness of their long separations.

Each time they had reunited after time apart, they'd seemed less in synch than before. He had to have noticed. She'd see him for the first time in months and forget to breathe as she thought, God, he's the most gorgeous man walking this earth.

She'd never met a man that exuded such raw sexuality wearing jeans and a T-shirt. But it had always been his eyes that had captivated her the most. They spoke even when he was silent.

Like the Ionian Sea, his irises were always changing color. But light was the driving force in the sea's color. The hour of the day, water depth and weather all changed the way it appeared to the eye. On the other hand, Karl's mood affected his eye color much more than the light of day.

The last time she greeted him at her front door, she saw none of the aquamarine radiance she'd remembered. She saw distant, deep water blue that showed his thoughts were troubled and that all the familiarity and intimacy between them had flown. In many ways, a

Navy SEAL was a free spirit. He had to be to live that kind of life. It didn't feel fair to entrap him when he no longer felt the same about her. She couldn't cling to the man she loved when it seemed all he wanted was to be free.

He should have thanked her for throwing out the *maybe we should date other people* idea or given some indication he wanted to salvage the relationship. Instead of the relieved response she'd expected, he had greeted her suggestion with stony silence and never called again. She had anticipated they'd at least remain friends. *So much for that plan.*

Too many nights, she'd fallen asleep in her office only to awaken with her face on the keyboard. She would jerk awake, wondering if the sound that had interrupted her slumber had been her ringing phone and the caller were Karl.

A thrill of excitement would jolt through her as she imagined hearing his deep, soothing voice on the other end of the line. Instead, she would grab her phone to see no calls displayed on the screen and soon realize the sound she'd gotten needlessly excited about had been a chime from an email or a beep from a smoke detector. Her silent phone would taunt her, making her feel more isolated and alone than ever.

She'd clung to her work like a lifeboat. It was the only thing keeping the loss of the relationship from pulling her underwater into a dark world of depression. She'd always been highly independent and had never felt the need to have a man in her life. Before moving to Paris, she'd dumped an overly critical boyfriend and hadn't dated anyone in France before or after Karl. She'd barely given relationships a second thought until recently.

Sure, Paris was a romantic city and from time to time she would see a couple kissing or with arms linked and feel a twinge or two of longing. After her relationship with Karl had ended, couples in love seemed to follow her everywhere. They locked lips in every café she frequented for a caffeine pick-me-up, exchanged saliva aboard every bus she caught to and from work, and pawed each other while she awkwardly gazed at her toes on a ride up an elevator.

The mingling of revulsion and longing she'd felt during these instances had confused her, making her wonder if she truly missed Karl or just the romantic illusion of being in love. She still wasn't sure. Sometimes she wondered if their entire relationship had been built on a foundation of adrenaline and a suspense movie like rescue. *Life isn't anything like what you see at the box office.*

Once the hero had rescued the damsel about to perish, the thrill could only last so long. *But still...* There had been a meant-to-be rightness about her and Karl as a couple that had lasted for months beyond that honeymoon week in Paris. *Maybe neither of us tried hard enough to make it work?* The last time he'd come to visit her, she'd worked late into the night more than once to polish a headline story. *I could have slowed down for a few days. Or taken vacation leave. Why was I so stubborn?*

Jamie slid open her patio door. The lush greenery on the island had caught her by surprise. The hillside where the hotel was perched and the rolling hills visible from where she stood were a dense forest of olive and fir trees.

The hill steeply descended to the beach, where the lapis blue Ionian Sea stretched out for miles, broken up only by forest green islands rimmed by white limestone and ended in the hazy distance, where the arid mountains of mainland Greece jutted up into the sky.

Wind snapped her hair back away from her face and whipped the hems of her long dress upward. The sea breeze made her imagine Karl's sensual hand smoothing over her shoulder, the tickle of his warm breath along her neck.

Annoyed by her runaway thoughts, she turned her back on the idyllic view and re-entered her room. She peeled off her sundress and tossed it onto a chair before slipping on a one-piece swimsuit.

Positioning one foot in front of the other and adopting a front stance, she launched into a routine of karate steps, punches, kicks and hand slices to work off her pent-up frustration. "Whoom," she said as she struck an empty ice bucket with a knife hand strike sending it flying through the air and bouncing across the floor. In her mind, that ice bucket was the head of the brunette Karl's eyes had been glued to.

You're nuts. She couldn't remember ever experiencing so much pent up frustration. She was breaking all the rules practicing what was supposed to be a disciplined art in an unruly rage. She'd been instructed to temper her anger, to maintain mental control of every movement. But she wasn't in control. She was completely crazed.

After thirty minutes of fighting the air like she wanted to kill it, sweat dripped from her body and she gasped for breath. The colorful photographs on the walls around her continued to dip and sway even after she stopped lashing out at her environment. A river of sweat dripped between her breasts and her hair hung in wet ringlets around her face. *This room feels like a sauna.* The box air conditioning unit just wasn't cutting it. Not that too many guests were likely to engage in crazed exercise in their rooms. Her exhausted thigh muscles barely supported her as she stumbled toward the shower. After a quick rinse, she wrapped a towel around her body, relishing the cooling sensation of still being wet.

She stepped out of the bathroom and looked longingly at the bed. *I'll just lie down for a minute or two.* She collapsed onto the soft mattress, nestled her dripping wet head into a pillow and instantly fell asleep.

CHAPTER FOUR

May 25, 2016
Nikiana Hotel
Lefkada Island, Greece
1430 hours

Nathan Brooks tossed back another swallow of warm beer before setting his glass on the counter of the poolside hotel bar. "Warm beer, inefficient, box-on-the-wall air-conditioning and hotter-than-hell weather. Why couldn't you get married in Alaska?" he teased.

"Because it's not romantic, that's why," said Nathan's best friend, Darryl. "The Greek islands are ideal for a destination wedding. How about if we take a boat out later? It's breezy out on the water, we'll fly over the waves and you'll get your adrenaline fix for the day."

"I'd be up for that," said Nathan.

The two had served together on DEVGRU until fifteen months ago when Nathan had resigned from his Navy duties due to a serious shoulder injury. After surgery and an extensive recovery and rehabilitation period, he had begun consulting for the U.S. Department of State. Nathan missed the excitement of back-to-back missions, but his new career was a better fit for his damaged rotator cuff muscles and love life.

Truth be told, the Mediterranean climate appealed to him, but he had no intention of letting Darryl know that so soon. Egging him on was far too entertaining.

"I still don't see how you figure hot is romantic. You two could have tied the knot in Somalia or Syria for a whole lot less money," Nathan joked. He'd spent far too much time in both countries recently. The Syrian and Somali deserts had been like saunas on steroids.

"Stop fucking with me. So it's ninety something degrees, but the island's beautiful and so are the beaches." Darryl's biceps flexed as he raised his beer glass and tossed back another swallow. "And for once, we're safe from the insurgents."

"Yeah, there is that." Nathan heard a distant roar that sounded like an airplane taking off before bottles above the bar shook and rattled. His barstool lilted from side to side making him feel as if he were onboard a boat experiencing the motion of waves. "What the hell?"

The bartender shrugged. "It's just a little quake. We have them here all the time. The Hellenic trench is just off the west coast."

"Heat and earthquakes." Nathan shook his head and smirked at Darryl.

Darryl set his glass down on the counter and laughed. "You high-maintenance independent workers can't handle a little mild discomfort?"

"Hey, I'm on vacation. I should be able to drink a cold beer without worrying the ground might swallow me up."

"Stop your belly aching and dive in the pool."

"You don't have to ask twice." Nathan chugged the rest of his beer and jumped up from the barstool. Peeling his shirt off mid-stride, he tossed it onto a lounge chair before diving into the deep end of the lagoon-shaped pool.

The cool water snapped his thoughts back into focus. After propelling himself underwater with pulls and kicks a full length of the pool, he surfaced and sucked in a deep breath as he stood in the waist-deep water. The hot breeze beaded the water on his upper torso. Blinking away water that blurred his vision, he glanced back to where they'd been sitting. Darryl had vacated his post to take a plunge and swam toward him doing a head-raised freestyle.

Darryl spoke as he stroked toward him. "The weather is perfect for the pool."

"I can't argue with that." The cool water refreshed his travel-weary body and even the arid, late summer breeze felt first-rate now that he was mostly submerged.

"So where's Olivia?"

"She went with her mom to Nidri to shop. She asked me if I wanted to go along, but I can't think of a worse way to spend the day than browsing through a bunch of shops. They wanted to look for olive oil cream and utensils made of olive wood. Doesn't that sound thrilling?"

"Shit, no."

"I won't see much of her this week since our mothers think the groom seeing the bride the day before the wedding is bad luck."

While Darryl excelled at following rules whether in the military or in day-to-day life, Nathan had always figured he followed enough goddamned rules at work and rebelled against customs and norms that seemed stupid to him. "Seriously? That sounds like a load of crap. How can you stand it? You've spent weeks apart."

Darryl's brows drew together and he gave Nathan a stern, unblinking look. "I know, Nathan. But in some ways a wedding is like a performance for the family."

It stunned Nathan that any man could find such a thing even remotely acceptable. "It sounds like it. What else is part of the show?"

"We are trying to preserve the romantic notions our moms have that we're saving ourselves for our wedding night and all that."

Nathan burst out laughing. "Fuckin' A. They really believe that?"

A wry smile curled up the corners of Darryl's mouth. "It seems so. We're also marrying on the half hour so the hands of the clock are moving up even though most clocks are digital these days."

All the hours of planning and having to be on stage in front of everyone seemed like enough of a sacrifice to Nathan. Eloping and telling all the fussy relatives they'd married after the fact seemed like a much saner idea than complying with a bunch of superstitious traditions. "Why the hell does that matter?"

"It's another one of those old time superstitions. If the hands are moving down, the marriage is supposed to be doomed or so they say."

"Jesus Christ," Nathan said so loud a middle-aged woman standing in the water nearby glanced his way. He leaned closer to

Darryl and lowered his voice. "As long as all this weird shit doesn't get to you, I guess it's good to keep the peace."

Darryl's stern expression made his dimples look deeper than ever on his tanned face. "One day of compromise isn't much of a sacrifice when we get to live our way for years after that. I just wish my dad could be here for this." He paused for a moment, his gaze looking reflective. "He wouldn't have said it to my face—he was never one to express emotions much—but I know he would have approved of my choice."

Nathan nodded. "Yeah, he would have. She's the one for you, man, that's for sure." There was no doubt Olivia was good for Darryl. The instant she walked into the room, Darryl's expression softened and he gazed at her in that completely smitten way.

In the year since their engagement, Darryl had only rarely experienced episodes of PTSD and had gained several pounds of muscle weight. Two days with Olivia in Greece and he looked relaxed and rested. "I'm really happy for you, man. You make a great couple."

Talking about Darryl's relationship got Nathan thinking of his girlfriend Baylee. He and the former Air Force Captain had been hot and heavy for two years and now shared a Connecticut condominium titled in both of their names. She'd embarked on her new career as an elementary school teacher in the Greenwich School District with flourish and still could drive him to the edge of insanity in bed.

Baylee could have done well for herself as an interior designer or handyman as was evident in all the home-improvement projects they'd embarked on together. Whether it was spreading a coating of thinset, laying ceramic tile or fixing a leaky sink or cranky toilet, she knew how to get the job done and do it right.

She often showed him the best way to do things. She also had a thing for loud colors and had sponge painted each room a different shocking color that had really brought their place to life. They'd made a sterile condominium into something pretty cool and life felt good whenever she was around. Maybe it was time he got around to making a commitment.

"Thanks for the kind words, Nathan. But stop will you? I'm tearing up over here."

"Tearing up my ass. I'm just calling it like I see it." The fiery Baylee was every bit as cut out for Nathan as Darryl and Olivia were for each other. The image of his platinum blonde-haired girlfriend's freckled pale face and mischievous smile popped into his mind, bringing a grin to his face.

She'd still been naked when he'd left the room, her face and skin flushed from a sweaty, lusty round of sex. She'd planned to run on the beach while he enjoyed a happy hour beer or three with his friend. He imagined she'd probably do pushups down there in the sand, too. He knew from experience, his Baylee had an arm on her.

Whenever he teased her, she'd slug him on his good shoulder. She was so strong sometimes an affectionate or playful punch left a bruise. If she were really pissed at someone, they'd be in serious trouble.

Nathan reprimanded himself for having gotten too comfortable with their domestic situation. He'd taken it for granted that they would stay together indefinitely and had postponed making the dreaded proposal he imagined he would pull off awkwardly at best.

It might be helpful to get Darryl to weigh in on the situation. He cleared his throat, intending to speak in a casual voice. He didn't want to sound too caught up in this. "I'm thinking about popping the question with Baylee."

Darryl splashed water in his direction and smiled. "Great idea, Nath. She knows how to keep you in line."

"Yeah, she does." Nathan cleared his throat, feeling uncomfortable. *Damn. Why didn't I bring up major league baseball instead?*

"So what's taken you so long? You don't have to ask my permission to go after what you want."

Nathan felt uncomfortable confessing his doubts. It wasn't a manly thing to do. "I don't know."

"Come on, man, just say it."

Nathan pushed his hands around in the water and looked away, unable to look Darryl in the eye. Confessions of weakness had never been his forte. "What if I fuck up the whole thing or she says *no*?"

"No way that will happen. When a woman's in love the way Baylee is with you, you buy her a ring, ask her to marry her and she bursts into happy tears. It's as simple as that. Why don't you ask her here on Lefkada? Women are always in a romantic mood at weddings and she'll never forget a Greek island proposal."

"I still think Alaska would be a more romantic place for a proposal. And a wedding."

Darryl launched water his way, splashing him in the face. "I'm sure Baylee wouldn't think so. Stop with the bullshit excuses and just do it."

"The time has to be right."

Darryl laughed and shook his head. "That was my plan in Prague so I waited days for the perfect time and you saw how that turned out."

Nathan would never forget that night when he and Baylee had met the couple for a post-dinner drink to learn that Darryl had just proposed and Olivia had accepted. Minutes later, Darryl's phone had rung and Chief Drake had deployed Darryl and several other DEVGRU members on an urgent mission. Instead of the planned celebration, Darryl had rushed to the airport to board a plane for Paris while Nathan—on medical leave with an injured shoulder—had remained in Prague.

"Have you bought her an engagement ring?"

"Yeah. Something caught my eye in a display window last week while I was at the mall grabbing some stuff for this trip."

"I hope you didn't get it from a gum ball machine."

Nathan rolled his eyes in exasperation. "Knock it off. I dropped two month's pay on the damn thing."

"Maybe you do have some class after all."

"Yeah, I do."

"You could walk her down to the beach, give her a kiss before you kneel in the sand and propose. It would be just like in the movies."

"I can figure it out." Why was his friend offering up all this unsolicited advice? He didn't need a fucking proposal coach. Did Darryl think he was a complete Neanderthal when it came to romance?

"So sorry I bruised your ego, dude, but it sounded like you needed a tip or two."

"Fine, I get it." It wasn't the end of the world that Darryl knew he was uptight. What frustrated him most was the possibility that he might actually need a shitload of advice. He didn't know a damn thing about romance. The ring selection experience had spotlighted that fact.

After the female sales clerk had frowned and shaken her head at his initial ring choice—a ring he had found to be both attractive and economical—he had texted his mother images of various rings he thought would be perfect.

His first choice had gleaned a "You've got to be kidding" response. An image of a ring that had cost a fortune and that he had found to be gaudy and old-fashioned looking had won his mom's approval.

Nathan sighed. *So I don't have good taste in rings.* Jewelry wasn't something enlisted men who could bench press two hundred and fifty pounds and were trained to use an array of powerful weapons should be experts in. *But if she ever wants a pistol for Christmas, I'll be great at picking that out.*

"Relax, I'm only trying to help."

"I know. But I can be romantic when I want to be. What if I slip on the ring and ask her right after a round or two of sweaty sex?"

"Are you out of your fucking mind? Baylee might bludgeon you to death if you make that move."

Nathan sighed. He only got one shot at this. He didn't want to fuck it up. "Fine. The beach it is." He flashed back to some of the corny chick flicks he'd suffered through over the years.

He would invite her to take a walk, acting very casual so she didn't suspect anything. He would take her hand as they strolled along the shore. And then just when she thought the purpose of the walk was exercise or watching a sunset, he would drop down onto the sand, gripping her other hand and facing her, gazing into her eyes and verbally admiring the beautiful way the sea breeze whipped through her hair before he asked her to spend the rest of her life with him. *That could work.*

Darryl's excited voice pulled him away from his reflections. "Look who's here?"

Two adults and two young kids approached the pool with towels draped over their shoulders. With a grin and a wave, Darryl waded toward the side of the pool to greet them.

Nathan plowed his way through the water to keep up. "Is that your brother and his family?" The man appeared to be a few years older than Darryl and shared his reddish brown hair and brilliant green eyes. The similarities ended there. The man's skin was glow-in-the-dark pale and he lacked Darryl's sturdy physique.

"You betcha. I'll introduce you to Kate and Phil here in a minute. And you'll love my niece and nephew. Talk about energy. Those two have a lot of it. I don't think either of them have an off switch. Once they meet you, they'll beg you to play pool games. Jonathon and Samantha are both great swimmers."

"Maybe your nephew will be a SEAL someday?"

"I'd much rather see the little guy become an Olympic swimmer. At least he'd have some chance at a normal life." Darryl pushed himself up out of the pool and greeted his family with warm enthusiasm.

Nathan climbed out of the water and stood beside Darryl waiting for the introductions.

After giving his brother a wet hug, Darryl introduced Nathan to his brother and family. Then he squatted down to speak to his niece and nephew at eye level. "Are you guys ready for a game of sharks and minnows?"

Jonathon and Samantha shrieked with excitement, skipping toward the edge of the pool behind him and jumping in with a splash. The four adults took a while longer to make their way to the water. Jonathon pointed at Darryl and shouted, "Uncle Darryl should be the shark."

"Yeah, Uncle Darryl, please?" asked Samantha, her green eyes wide and pleading.

Darryl's smile made it clear his loud groan was fake. "You two swim like fish. I'll never be able to catch you."

"Don't worry, you'll be able to catch my dad," said Jonathon in a serious tone of voice, his eyes widening. "He's got lots of fat around his stomach so he won't be able to move very fast."

Kate reprimanded her son for the inappropriate comment.

Jonathon burst out with a quick *sorry* and then performed a splashy flip in the water.

After deciding to start in the water to reduce the risk of the excited kids slipping on the deck, the group positioned themselves along the wall and waited for Darryl to kick off the game.

A man's loud, heavily accented voice caught by surprise. "Excuse me, are you Nathan Brooks?"

"Yes, that's me." He swung around to face the man who had spoken.

Creases marred the dark-skinned man's forehead. Sweat dripped from his coal black hair and sweat dripped from the drenched button up shirt he wore. The guy looked like he had run miles in his street clothes. "I have come here to deliver a message."

"What kind of message?" The relaxed beer haze vaporized as Nathan's *something's not right with this picture* antenna kicked his body into ready mode. He tried to spot what the man held behind his back. *A pistol? A semi-automatic? A knife? Just let him try to hurt me.* His muscles contracted and his mind readied for attack. *A fist to the face, a simultaneous grab of the weapon, then a twist to break the wrist should do the trick.*

When the man's hands swung around to the front of his body, they displayed an envelope instead of a weapon.

Nathan's muscles relaxed. Maybe his credit card had been denied and this was a summary of his hotel bill so far? He'd forgotten to notify the bank about his travel plans. *Or it could be anthrax.*

Nathan's training had taught him to never let his guard down. When men in his position stopped suspecting anything and everything might be a threat, they often ended up a corpse or in a shit load of trouble.

"It is a very urgent kind of message," the man said, a smile twisting his lips. "I suggest you read it right away." The envelope landed with a splat on the wet pool deck before the man turned and strode briskly toward the path leading to the beach.

Nathan climbed out of the pool and shouted, "Wait. Who are you and what is this all about?"

He walked across the hot deck in his bare feet and jerked to a stop once he reached the winding stone and sand trail that dropped steeply toward the beach. "Damn it."

The man had broken into a run and dropped out of sight, obscured by the thick grove of cypress and olive trees that surrounded the trail. A fast runner, Nathan knew he could catch the man if he wanted to, but decided reading the message was top priority.

Shaking his head, Nathan walked back over to where the envelope lay. The man delivering it hadn't worn gloves or a mask so he assumed it was safe to touch. He crouched down and picked up the dampened parcel, sliding a finger under the sealed flap to rip it open.

"You weren't supposed to get out of the water, Nathan," Samantha said defiantly, her eyes large with dismay. "Because you cheated, now you have to be the shark."

Nathan was determined to make light of the situation for now, even though he sensed a threat. Causing needless alarm wouldn't do anyone any good. "You're right, Samantha. Normally, I always follow the rules. That man brought me some mail and I needed to speak to him."

Samantha lips stretched into a doubtful frown and her youthful green eyes gazed at him intently, as if trying to determine if he was lying or not. Clearly, she wasn't going for his answer. "Why did he run away? It didn't look like he wanted to talk to you."

"He, uh, had more mail to deliver and was in a hurry," Nathan stumbled out awkwardly. Having to fib to Darryl's sharp-minded niece wasn't something he'd ever anticipated. *But what choice do I have?* "How about this. I'll read my mail real quick and then be the shark. Is that okay?"

She looked at her brother and when he nodded, she answered, "I guess that will be okay." She performed a handstand on the bottom of the pool, kicking her legs in the air.

Darryl tapped her on the shoulder when she surfaced. "Samantha why don't you be the shark for now while I talk to Nathan," said Darryl. "We'll get back in the game real soon." He strode through the water toward Nathan with a clenched jaw.

"I thought that guy was going to pull a gun for a minute," Darryl said in a hushed voice once he reached the side of the pool.

"Yeah, me too. The whole incident was odd. I've got a bad feeling about this."

"Don't just stare at it. Open the damn thing," Darryl said impatiently.

Still crouched on the pool deck, Nathan slid the note out from the envelope and unfolded it. His eyes scanned over the text and as its meaning struck home, his heart thundered inside his rib cage. *This can't be happening.* "Jesus Christ, no."

"What is it?" Darryl snatched the note from Nathan's hand.

Nathan didn't wait for his friend's reaction. He pushed himself out of the pool and ran across the deck for his towel and flip-flops.

Darryl leaped from the pool and rushed to his side, the note still clipped between his fingers and blowing in the afternoon breeze. "Tell me what's going on."

"I don't want to talk now. Just come with me, okay? I've got to get to the room ASAP." Nathan grabbed his room key, not bothering to pull on his shirt.

Darryl unfolded the note, scanned over it quickly, and swore.

"What is it, Uncle Darryl?" Jonathon asked, jumping up and down in the pool and splashing water with his hands. "Are we playing a different game now?"

Darryl clenched his jaw and spoke, sounding amazingly calm. "No, buddy. We've got a problem related to our work."

Phil climbed out of the pool and strode toward them, planting his hands on his hips. "Your work? Will you two stop it? You're scaring my kids."

Darryl placed a hand on his brother's shoulder. "I'm not messing with you, Phil. We've got a problem. Until we get back, stay alert and don't let those kids out of your sight for a second."

"Damn, you're serious, aren't you? I wish you would tell us—"

"I will when I can." The second Darryl tipped his head toward the building indicating he was ready; Nathan turned and sprinted down the stone path.

CHAPTER FIVE

May 25, 2016
Nikiana Hotel
Lefkada Island, Greece
1455 hours

After plumping up the lumpy pillow, Jamie had collapsed onto the too firm mattress and allowed her heavy eyelids to flutter shut. *I'm so exhausted* was her last conscious thought. A loud bang broke into her slumber. A door being kicked down or a piece of furniture being thrown at the wall? She fought to open her eyes, but her eyelids refused to budge. They felt leaden, weighed down. Gravity seemed to be mocking her.

Something's wrong. She fought harder, straining her eyelids open to see a beach of bone white sand. *What am I doing out here?* She felt confused.

Last thing she remembered she'd been sprawled out on her hotel room bed. She squinted and raised a hand in front of her face to block out the blinding sunlight. The sand between her toes singed her feet. *Why didn't I wear shoes?* She couldn't even remember having walked down to the beach. *How weird. I must be spacey because of the jet lag.*

Craving relief from the heat that scorched her skin from every angle, she stepped toward the edge of the Ionian Sea. The water in the protected cove was calm and clear as crystal. She could see rounded stones and sand on the bottom of the shallow water. Gentle waves lapped at the sand.

She waded knee deep into the sea. Her pale feet appeared slightly larger beneath the crystal clear water. A small school of silver fish swam by her legs. When she took a step back, they jerked in a different direction and continued swimming in a straight line.

I wonder what other critters are in this water. The high tourist season hadn't yet begun. With few bathers in the water to scare them off, Jamie imagined sharks might venture close to shore.

Her shark worries were forgotten when she heard a high-pitched scream. Jamie whirled around to see a blonde-haired woman scratching and clawing at an assailant with bulging biceps. Her captor quickly overpowered her and pulled her arms behind her back. His eyes dark and crazed, his lips were twisted into an angry sneer.

"Let me go, you bastard." The frightened woman grunted and jerked her body around, her fair skin flushing red as she strained to free herself from the man's grasp.

Wait, that can't be... Incensed, Jamie tried to open her mouth to reprimand the assailant, but her lips wouldn't move. She willed her body to sprint toward the woman, but her limbs seemed paralyzed as well. *Damn it.* She realized she was trapped in a dream.

She hated dreams where she was helpless and out-of-control. Asleep or awake, Jamie was used to leaping into the action. *Please let me wake up.*

The scene she seemed helpless to engage in continued to play out in front of her eyes. Invisible hands bound every muscle in her body. *Damn it. Damn it. Damn it.*

Holding the blonde woman tight enough with one hand to keep her from escaping, the man reached in his pocket with the other hand and pulled a bandana from his pocket.

"They'll track you down, you basta—" the woman shouted in a defiant voice before he wrapped the gag so tightly around her head, it cut into the edges of her mouth.

The sinister man released a haunting laugh that sent tingles prickling up Jamie's spine. "Oh, yes, I'll make sure your paid-by-the-job boyfriend and his Navy SEAL friends are informed of your absence. They will think twice about disrupting our organization's activities after I'm finished with you. Welcome to Greece. A few hours in the bowels of the *Ionian Gypsy* will be the beginning of your day's itinerary. A long and painful death will conclude your travels."

The woman jabbed him in the gut with her elbow. Infuriated, the man struck the back of her head hard with the side of his hand. The woman's features slackened, her eyeballs rolled upward and she dropped onto the sand like a limp rag.

You bastard. Jamie tried to force a scream from her lips to no avail. Her paralysis infuriated her. Her mind screamed and thrashed. Please, I have to wake up. Her strong will battled to escape the confining walls of the nightmare.

Suddenly, she sensed the press of the hard mattress against her spine, the support of a pillow behind her head. *Thank God, I'm awake. That was terrifying.* Her body trembling, her skin damp with cold sweat, she jerked her eyelids open, sat up in bed and tried to reorient herself.

I'm in my room in Greece. And my only worry is avoiding Karl.

A distressed male voice from a neighboring room ripped through the silence. "Baylee. Baylee. Fuck, where have they taken her?"

CHAPTER SIX

May 25, 2016
Nikiana Hotel
Lefkada Island, Greece
1455 hours

Nathan had sprinted at a break neck pace back to his hotel unit, not caring about the people he plowed into on the way. Getting to Baylee had been his one and only priority. After dashing up the stairs to the second story and down the hall, he found his room door ajar. *God damn it.* He shoved the door open and shouted her name again and again.

He had expected to find her missing, but seeing the evidence of the violent skirmish that had taken place minutes ago between Baylee and her captors caused him to burst into expletives.

The blue curtains had been thrown open, casting blinding light into the room. The wooden chairs and a small table in front of the sofa had been overturned and broken glass was scattered across the tile floor. One chair had a splintered leg.

Nathan imagined Baylee grabbing it, swinging it wildly in the air and trying to crash it over the head of her assailant. He'd learned within minutes of meeting her that her fragile appearance was a major contradiction to her personality. Clearly, his feisty Baylee had put up one hell of a fight. *I wish she'd brained that bastard.*

He clenched his fists and ground his teeth together. *Once I get my hands on him, I'll rip him into shreds.* Frowning, he knelt down and studied the blood spatters on the white tile floor. A punch in the nose, a scrape against a piece of splintered wood? *Or maybe the bastard cut her.*

Pain seared his heart. Finding her missing had cut him bad, but seeing the evidence that the woman he loved had been injured or worse further cauterized his emotional wound. He clenched his fists and jumped to his feet, wanting to punch a hole through a wall, to inflict some kind of physical damage on an inanimate object to relieve the anger building up inside of him. "Damn it, Darryl. I can't believe she's gone. Why would they take her instead of me? If only I knew what they wanted, maybe I could negotiate with them." He spoke those words knowing fully that negotiating with terrorists was a lost cause and that the note had spelled out exactly what they wanted. They wanted revenge.

Darryl stopped his perusal of the room to look at him. "You think the Muslim Alliance is responsible for this?"

"I'm sure of it."

Four months earlier…

Nathan had been deployed on a top priority mission on January 24, 2016. Two SEAL Teams, the best of the Deltas, CIA, FBI and contract hires, including Nathan, had been called in for the emergency briefing at the Pentagon with the President of the United States, the Defense Secretary and National Security Advisor.

"The Muslim Alliance has to be stopped," said the Defense Secretary. "The other insurgencies we've dealt with have mostly been restricted to the Middle East and North Africa, places most Americans avoid. The MA's method of terror is causing widespread panic. The Dow has tumbled more than five hundred points again today. After the drastic dips the past two weeks, investors are panicking.

Frightened people sell stocks and hoard money. The American economy is going to collapse if people don't stop pulling money out of the stock market. To turn things around, we have to end the fear, get people traveling again or at least leaving their homes."

The Defense Secretary went on to cite instances of kidnappings and consequent grisly executions of United States citizens. When hostages were executed, it wasn't simply recorded and posted online.

Instead, this sophisticated network of insurgents had found ways to hack into prime-time television stations and post autoplay videos on social media so unsuspecting viewers saw a person's head cut off with a blade, someone shot dozens of time with an automatic weapon or even held underwater until they drowned.

In the past, people who didn't have a thirst for watching violence could avoid being exposed to these violent clips. It wasn't even safe to kick back in an easy chair with a beer to watch a ball game anymore or for kids coming home from school to watch sitcoms or cartoons. Anytime someone flipped on the TV or visited social media sites, there was a possibility that terrifying violence would flash up on the screen.

Many of the victims of these grisly executions had traveled to countries deemed safe by the State Department. England, Greece, Spain, Ireland. Now nearly every country's listing was scarred by terror warnings. Two Americans had been executed on Caribbean islands in the past month and the previous day a woman had been beheaded in front of hundreds of witnesses in a San Francisco shopping center.

People had begun to hoard food and hide out in their homes, leaving only for work and essential activities. Movie theaters and malls were on the brink of bankruptcy.

"IT specialists have hacked into the underground network and penetrated the recruiting channels. We've got people working to shut the terror networks down in the States, but we need a large team to do some damage abroad where all this originates.

"That's where you people come in." The Defense Secretary outlined his plan to have them infiltrate the organization, rescue hostages and take out targets. "We have to make an impact in a hurry. It's essential that we convince the American people that it's safe to live again. But it isn't going to be an easy task."

Hundreds of CIA operatives were being sent to various locations to infiltrate the organization. Snipers were being sent with special ops squads to eliminate targets.

Nathan had been assigned to work with a team of elite military to rescue an American couple being held hostage in an Aruba hotel.

"According to reliable intel, their execution will take place in twenty eight hours. Colonel Baker will lead you on this series of missions."

A stern man in uniform nodded and stepped to the front of the room to address the group. "We'll be moving out within the hour. This isn't going to be an extract and go home mission. We've got a whole series of rescues planned.

"Don't expect to be drinking Mai Tais for long in the Caribbean or returning Stateside for a break. Most of our other extraction missions will take us to Middle East and North Africa.

"It's imperative that we inflict major damage to their reputation in a short amount of time and we're not going to accomplish that sleeping. We've got detailed photographs taken from inside the Aruba hotel so this mission should be a cakewalk, a good warm-up for what's to come. But at some point, they're going to suspect we've got people planted in the organization. That's when these missions are going to get ugly."

Yeah, that's for fucking sure. Nathan wished he could be working with his DEVGRU Team on something this dicey instead of a group of men he'd never met until today. He had to hope to hell his stern superior and the rest of these people would have his back when the mission went haywire.

It had been the eighth hostage extraction rescue they'd performed in less than seventy-two hours. The Black Hawk had hovered over a rocky promontory above the village of Dumar, northwest of Damascus in the dead of night.

After fast roping from the copter to the ground, Nathan and the others rappelled down the cliffs, waded across the Barada River and crept, dripping wet into the city. Bleached white buildings glowed bright green through his night vision goggles.

Three men in their group roped their way up onto nearby rooftops, readying their weapons to fire at hostiles. Nathan's muscles tensed and his mind and senses became heightened by the adrenaline racing through his blood stream.

He spotted a guard with an automatic weapon standing outside the main entrance to the ten-story apartment building and reported the siting to the Colonel. Their leader remained in a safe location a distance away, watching the scene through a camera.

The Colonel spoke to the team through the headsets. "Put the Tango out of commission, Brooks."

"Copy that, sir." Nathan aimed his silencer-enhanced weapon toward its target and fired.

After taking a bullet to the head, the man silently slumped to the ground. *So far so good.*

"The front door's been unlocked by another resident in advance of our visit. Entry should be a cakewalk," said the Colonel.

Nathan pulled the heavy metal door open and the other men in his squad rushed into the building behind him. Keeping his fingers curled around the trigger, his senses alert to sudden movements or sounds, he stealthily walked past the elevator toward the stairs. He pointed down the hallway toward a door he knew, from studying the building layout, led to the stairwell.

One loud footfall or heavy breath would echo through the high-ceilinged cement structure and devastate their sneak attack. He controlled his breathing and tried not to make a sound as he stealthily walked up the nine flights of stairs toward the target floor.

Sweat mingled with the muddy river water that saturated his uniform. His nose itched like hell, but he refused to scratch it. All his attention had to be directed toward one cause; extracting the hostages alive. He halted in front of apartment nine hundred eighteen.

"Pick the lock, but try not to make too much noise," the Colonel said.

Nathan pulled out his kit of tools that combined with a deft hand could overpower every kind of lock in existence. He stuck one metal instrument into the opening and jiggled, gritting his teeth at the eruption of scratching sounds that seemed to echo through the hallway. He knew sounds seemed magnified to him when he was on edge. Just stay calm, he told himself, while he wished the kidnappers were watching television or listening to a radio or engaged in some noise-producing activity that would block out the efforts of his forced entry.

He held his breath as the lock began to release. *Almost there.* His mind jumped ahead to the next phase of their operation. He knew there were two bedrooms in the apartment and a couple and their ten-year-old son were being held prisoner in the one furthest from the door.

Were they sleeping or awake? Was a guard standing behind the door, waiting for Nathan to swing it open so he could shoot him and the others at point-blank range?

There wasn't time for second-guessing. He had a job to do and he had to be ready for anything. I'm on top of this, he told himself after one lock released. *One more and we're in.*

He punched the metal into the second lock.

The Colonel's voice pierced through his earpiece and reverberated inside his head. "What's taking you so goddamn long?"

Nathan didn't answer. He didn't dare make a sound. The hallway smelled of dust and sour urine. He gritted his teeth as the impulse to sneeze seized him. *Fuck, no.* He pushed an elbow to the underside of his nose to stop the impulse. Two more jiggles and the lock released. He gave a *thumbs up* sign that the Colonel would be able to see from the camera he wore on his helmet, clenched his fingers around the trigger of his weapon and pulled open the door.

The apartment appeared neat and orderly through the dim green light his night vision goggles provided. A couch and two chairs were angled in toward the center of the square living room, a wide screen television had been mounted on one wall and books on a floor-to-ceiling bookshelf had been arranged shortest to tallest. The coffee table in front of the couch was empty.

No beer cans, no empty glass, no magazines. *Neat freak terrorists.* He hoped to hell the family had been treated as delicately as the unadorned apartment.

He'd been briefed to advance to the kitchen to make sure no one hid there before proceeding to the bedroom. The team of men found it empty and undisturbed. The sink was clear of dishes; the counters were slick and clean.

He craned his head and motioned for the six other men to follow him down the hallway toward the two bedrooms. The most difficult part of their task awaited them. Civilians weren't used to seeing men smeared with body paint, wearing night vision goggles and carrying Rambo-style weapons. The instant they saw the men, they'd freeze in terror, maybe even scream.

Nathan pulled the small American flag from his pants pocket that had a tiny light attached to illuminate it and stuck it in his lapel pocket. He heard the other men shuffling to do the same. This simple method had calmed victims more than once. *What if it doesn't work tonight?*

Nathan turned the knob and pulled the door open. When he stepped inside the room, gunfire erupted behind him. A woman screamed.

"I've been hit," shouted one of the men in Nathan's squad.

"Mother fuckers," a soldier shouted before several rounds of automatic weapon fire erupted all around.

Nathan heard the woman again, voicing what each of the Americans must have been thinking at that moment.

"Oh, my God, we're going to die. We're going to die."

Nathan hugged the wall beside the door, his eyes trained for movement. He swung the barrel of his weapon around, aiming at the shadow stepping through the door. Seeing enough of his outline to tell he wasn't friendly, he fired. The man dropped to the floor. He walked over to where the family sat on the floor, arms and ankles bound. "Stay low to the ground until this ends. We're here to get you out."

"What the hell is going on?" The Colonel's booming voice nearly deafened Nathan's left ear through the headset.

More staccatos of gunfire erupted. Another body crumpled to the floor. Nathan heard the front door open and the sound of footsteps sprinting down the hallway. He hoped to hell it was the back up team.

The woman's sobbing intensified.

"It's going to be okay," said a male voice. "I think American soldiers have come to rescue us."

"Maybe they're Deltas." The teenage boy captive sounded excited as well as scared.

"We're American operatives. We'll get you out. Please, stay calm. I need to assist the injured men on my squad," said Nathan.

"John's dead," said a Delta named Brian.

"Damn." Nathan strode across the room and out the door to study the damage. Blood gushed from John's chest. Men often died on missions, but that never made it easier the next time. Nathan reported the fatal shooting and the fact that two other men had been hit.

"Are the hostages okay?" the Colonel asked.

"Yeah, they're unharmed."

"Bring the hostages and injured men to the pick up point and we'll do the best we can to bandage the guys until we can get them treated."

Once the hostages had been released and led from the apartment, Nathan surveyed the apartment one last time. A voice that sounded more specter than human caused him to swing his body around. "You're going to pay for the damage you've done. You'll see."

The skin on Nathan's neck prickled. A man lay prone on the entryway floor and was slowly crawling toward him. He dropped to his knees and aimed his Sig Sauer at the man's forehead.

He couldn't wait to pull the trigger, to end the bloody bastard's life. "What do you want? These people are innocent. What good does it do you to murder them in cold blood?"

The man's face was bloody, his eyes crazed. "Violent death," he said in a haunting voice, the tenor of his voice rising to a terrifying crescendo. "We want violent death for all Americans. We know who you are, Nathan Brooks. You couldn't handle DEVGRU so now you're doing dirty work for the highest bidder."

"Yeah, whatever you say." Nathan ground his teeth together as he spoke, willing his voice to disguise his unease.

"You'll be talking differently when we have Baylee Stiles hog tied with a rifle held to her head."

The mention of Baylee's name sent Nathan into a frenzy of rage. His vision blurred and his face burned hot. "Shut the fuck up you bastard," Nathan shouted before he fired several rounds into the man's body. It bounced up off the floor before falling inert and bloody on the tile floor in front of him.

CHAPTER SEVEN

May 25, 2016
Nikiana Hotel
Lefkada Island, Greece
1500 hours

"Nathan, calm down and tell me what you're thinking. What makes you think the MA's responsible?"

"On my last mission a man we encountered during the extraction mission knew me by name. He knew more than that. He knew things about my personal life. Just before I killed the bastard, he mentioned Baylee. Said they were going to tie her up and hurt her. Those people know who we are, man. And they're after revenge."

"Did you report the incident to your superiors?"

"Damn straight. But they didn't take me too seriously. Said enough of a fatal blow had been delivered to the organization that it was in its death throes anyway. But optimism isn't something people like us can afford to have. Fucking hell, how are we going to get her back?" Despair rang in his voice. Every time he thought about what those men might be doing to Baylee, pain ripped through his insides.

"Obviously, your work has stirred up a hive of angry bees, but I don't get how your cover was blown. So much effort goes into keeping our identities secret. Our team's been after these bastards in recent months. I'm wondering what they know about the rest of us."

Nathan gave Darryl a wry smile. "I was just thinking the same thing. I'm guessing maybe someone who infiltrated the organization was tortured and talked." He told him what he knew about CIA agent Barry Sellock's mission.

He had been one of several agents sent to infiltrate the MA and provide intel to Colonel Baker. Nathan hoped Sellock's identity hadn't been compromised. He approached the most adverse operations with a joke and a smile. If the mild-mannered Sellock had been executed, his final moments weren't something Nathan wanted to imagine. MA terrorists gave a whole new meaning to the word *ruthless*.

"Sellock and the undercover people aren't given much information about DEVGRU because of the nature of our work. I think it's more likely someone within MA hacked into confidential files or tracked one of us."

Nathan wasn't privy to the details of DEVGRU missions anymore except on the rare occasions he worked side by side with them. But MA had been the most imminent recent threat and Darryl had implied the team had been up to their eyeballs dealing with them. "This is so fucked up. I wish I could contact the Colonel to find out if he's aware of any recent security breaches."

As it stood, he wasn't authorized to contact anyone. If his superiors at the State Department wanted to contact him, they did. It didn't work the other way around.

"I'll call in some support, don't worry."

"Are you sure that's our best option? Civilians are in danger here. Maybe everyone attending the wedding should be evacuated to a secure location?"

"Nath, I'm not leaving until we extract Baylee safely. Anyway, running isn't our best move. An evacuation would alarm our families and attract too much attention. Let me make some calls."

Darryl ran a finger over the leg of an overturned table before reaching into his pocket for his cell phone. "I'll contact Drake first. If there are FBI operatives or Delta Force guys in the area, he can send them over to examine evidence and offer us and our families additional protection. I'll also advise him of the security breach."

Nathan walked aimlessly around the room feeling dazed and disoriented. *How could things have gotten so fucked up so fast?* One minute, he'd been planning to propose to Baylee, the next he'd learned she'd been kidnapped. He'd gotten in the way of MA's prime objectives and now he was paying a bitter price.

He had often contemplated the possibility of sudden death on a mission, but had never considered that someone close to him might be targeted. He'd always taken it for granted that his identity would remain secret. Now that security blanket had been snatched away in a second.

It had been a major slip up not following normal security protocols when traveling to Greece. Although in the past he'd traveled on a commercial jet upon occasion, he'd also registered in a hotel in Athens using his real passport rather than a fake identity. If he'd been followed, the kidnappers might have seen him with Darryl, Olivia, Baylee and Karl. *Fuck, what a mess this is.*

He unfolded the off-white piece of stationary and read it again, feeling the urge to rip it into a million pieces.

Dear Mr. Brooks (and yes, we know that is your real name),

I have taken Ms. Baylee Stiles to an undisclosed location. Your recent interference with our activities has interrupted the accomplishment of our objectives as supported by Allah. At this moment Ms. Stiles is in very good health. Unfortunately, she must suffer and soon die so that you will be taught not to interfere with our plans again.

Sincerely,

Mr. A.

Mr. Asshole's more like it. "God damn it." Nathan threw the paper across the room, seething with anger.

Darryl recovered the paper and tried to comfort his friend before busying himself with a call to Chief Drake.

There would be no negotiating with these fuckers. How could people affiliated with this terrorist organization declare they were true Muslims? That they did the will of Allah? Most of MA recruits were atheists, people who believed in nothing, had given up on all hope and were willing and ready to die for any cause that gave their miserable lives some distorted sense of purpose.

MA's main aim was to instill fear and shock with their acts of violence. Terrorizing people was how these narrow-minded individuals sought to gain control and bring ruin to America, the country they believed responsible for all ills. Somehow the organization had uncovered their identities, found out about Darryl's wedding and planned to make a mess of it. *What else do these bastards have up their sleeves?*

He picked up a pale green tank top that had been draped over a chair and drew it toward his nostrils, inhaling Baylee's lingering fresh, citrusy scent. God, how he wished he could hold her tight in his arms at this moment and that this hellish kidnapping had never happened. Darryl's voice broke into his thoughts.

"Drake said FBI agents and Delta Force are stationed on Meganisi Island. They're mobilizing as we speak and will arrive by boat within the hour. He's also been in contact with the Greek police. They'll be here any minute to stake out the hotel and secure this room. The Deltas have been advised of our credentials and will supply us with weaponry when they arrive."

"Thanks, Darryl. I feel better knowing all this back up is on the way. When should we expect the Deltas to arrive?"

"Their anticipated arrival is fifteen thirty hours."

"Let's just hope they have a plan to help us rescue Baylee. Right now we've got nothing to go on."

"We're going to find her, Nathan. I'm one hundred percent committed to this." His gaze drifted toward the tank top Nathan held in his hands. "We shouldn't touch anything. Everything in this room is evidence. Let's head to the dock to meet the Deltas."

Nathan gently replaced the tank top over the back of the chair, took once last look around the room and sighed. "Damn it, Darryl. I can't stand playing this waiting game. Those bastards have Baylee and they're planning to kill her."

CHAPTER EIGHT

May 25, 2016
Nikiana Hotel
Lefkada Island, Greece
1510 hours

Jamie yawned and raised her arms over her head to stretch her aching limbs, feeling groggy and disoriented. The sleep deprivation she'd inflicted on herself for months had caught up with her. She rolled to the side of the bed, pushing herself to her feet. The towel knotted around her body loosened and slipped to the floor. Her still wet hair dripped onto her naked shoulders.

The commotion in the adjacent room continued, making her wonder if what she'd just dreamed had actually happened. Noises such as thunder, wind, and dogs barking had sometimes ended up in her dreams. She'd even had dreams where she'd needed to pee real bad and awoken to feel the same urge. *Maybe someone's really been kidnapped.*

Her ears piqued with interest at the words FBI and Delta Force. In a hurry to learn what was going on, she rummaged in her backpack for a fresh cotton dress and quickly pulled it over her head. After slipping on sandals and combing her fingers through her damp, tangled hair, she exited the room.

One of the blue-painted doors across the hall had been pulled open. She strode toward the opened door and peered inside to see Darryl and Nathan wearing stern expressions and shifting anxiously on their feet. Two men wearing Navy Blue uniforms and leg armor were sifting through debris on the room floor and placing them in plastic bags. *The Hellenic Police? They're looking for evidence... Evidence of what?*

Unable to control her journalistic instincts, Jamie barged in and burst out with, "What's going on? I heard a lot of noise from my room." She cast her gaze around the room, noticing it matched the cheerful, bright decor of her own accommodations with its white and gray tile floor pleasantly accented with lime green and sea blue furniture and accessories. The blue curtains bracketing the large window beside the double bed with the lime green bedspread and the sliding door adjacent to the blue sofa had been pulled open wide, casting bright light on the disturbing scene in front of her. A pale wooden table and two chairs had been overturned and fragments of what had once been a lime green glass were scattered across the floor.

The two police officers' heads snapped toward her. The thirty-something man with his tanned, Mediterranean complexion, thick, dark brows, large dark eyes and athletic body was handsome enough to melt a woman's eyeballs. His gaze wandered appreciatively over her physique.

Taking advantage of the man's interest in her, Jamie flipped her wet hair back from her face and spoke in a flirtatious voice. "You two men must be police officers."

"Yes, beautiful lady, that is ri—" said the young man in a sensual, accented voice.

The older man interrupted his companion and shot her a stern look, exaggerating the wrinkles on his sun and age-worn face. "This is a crime scene, Miss. You need to exit the room right away."

Jamie frowned and planted her hands on her hips. She had no intention of leaving until she knew what had happened. "I just want to know what's going on." She glanced at the handsome police officer and winked. "I'm Jamie Phillips by the way."

The young police officer's bicep muscles flexed and the corners of his full lips curled up in a disarming smile as he extended his hand toward her. "What a pleasure it is to meet you. I'm Officer Karahalios."

When their hands met, his grip was firm and he held on to her hand longer than necessary during the handshake. "Officer Laskaris here is my uncle. I would be really honored if you would call me Nicolaos."

"Oh, I see. Maybe I could do that." Jamie pulled her hand away, feeling uncomfortable with the gorgeous man's overt attention.

Nathan shook his head and gave both of them a dark look. "What the hell is this? The dating game?"

"I'm sorry, b—"

"We're on duty, remember?" After shaking his head at his nephew, Officer Laskaris turned toward Jamie. His dark eyebrows pulled together as he glanced at her still-dripping, tangled hair. "We have no time to converse with hotel guests. We're collecting evidence on a missing person's case. You must l—"

"Missing person? Who's missing?" The pitch of her voice rose. Her innately curious personality wouldn't settle for not knowing. She threw Darryl a pleading look. He had to remember that she'd disarmed a terrorist in the

Paris airport. He had been annoyed by her blatant interference, but he'd seen for himself she was a broadcast journalist gifted with skills they'd benefitted from in the end. Maybe he'd say it was safe to at least fill her in on the basics.

Darryl raised his hand in the air. "Don't worry, officer. She's a well known Paris broadcast journalist. She was on the scene with us during one of our recent missions."

"Fine, she can stay, but I don't want any information leaked to the press that I don't authorize. Is that clear?"

Jamie vigorously nodded her head. Typing up a headline story wasn't her biggest priority. Figuring out what the hell was happening was at the top of her list.

Nathan's steel blue eyes looked haunted as he spoke in an emasculated voice. "Baylee's been kidnapped."

"Oh, no. That's terrible." She'd met Baylee after the terrorist incident in Paris. She had feasted on boeuf bourguignon that night she and Karl had met up with Nathan, Baylee and Darryl for dinner and wine.

Baylee had shown herself to be outspoken and intelligent as the evening unfolded and bottle after bottle of wine had been poured. One thing Jamie knew for sure: Baylee wasn't a woman to be messed with.

Jamie glanced around the room, giving a more detailed perusal to the evidence of the brutal struggle. Images of her frightening nightmare flashed through her brain. The blond-haired woman in her dream had resembled Baylee. Even her voice had had the same defiant ring to it. *Everything in the dream really did happen.* "Did they leave a ransom note?"

"You could call it that, yes. Darryl and I were playing pool games with his niece and nephew when a strange man delivered an envelope containing a threatening note. We rushed back to the room and found her gone. So far the police haven't found any trace of fingerprints or any other evidence of consequence. We're waiting for FBI and Delta Force to arrive." Nathan's normally easy-going voice rang with frustration and despair.

Jamie wondered why Baylee had been the target. Maybe Nathan or Darryl had a hunch. "Do you have any idea who took her?"

"Yeah, we do. I can't go into details, but we suspect a terrorist organization. The message I received states that her captors plan to kill her. The worst part is that we have no leads as to where they've taken her."

"I think I know where she is," said Jamie.

All four men jerked their heads in her direction.

CHAPTER NINE

May 25, 2016
Nikiana Hotel
Lefkada Island, Greece
1520 hours

"Did you overhear the kidnapping?" Nathan's dark brows drew together.

"Sort of." Jamie shifted uneasily on her feet.

Nathan's muscles tensed and irritation rang in his voice. "What do you mean *sort of*? Either you heard the bastards or you didn't."

Jamie let out a long sigh before speaking. "I'm sorry, Nathan. Just hear me out, okay?" The sea of stern doubtful expressions was more than a little intimidating.

"I'm listening."

She cleared her throat, trying to picture herself in Nathan's predicament. A naturally compassionate person, Jamie found it easy to empathize with others. She would have been frantic and in tears had Karl been taken. She would have been starved for any scrap of information that might help her find him no matter how strange it sounded.

Why are you thinking about him *now? If something bad happened to Karl, why would you care? You're not together any more.* Her logic failed to persuade her runaway heart. It insisted that nothing could be worse than learning harm had come his way.

"I was asleep. I had a terrible nightmare about a woman being kidnapped. Only after I awoke and heard all the commotion did I realize my nightmare had really been hap—"

"Tell us everything you heard." Nathan's riveted gaze and the urgent tenor of his voice suggested he was on board with her story.

"I heard a woman screaming and trying to escape a captor. I'm not one hundred percent sure everything in my dream actually happened, but that's what I remember," explained Jaime.

Nathan brushed a hand over his chin and acknowledged her with a slow nod. "You don't have to convince me. I had a dream our team was being attacked once and awoke to find out terrorists had just blown the door to the compound where we were hiding out. Please tell us exactly what you heard."

"The woman in my dream put up one hell of a fight. She kicked, screamed, and attacked her assailant with colorful expletives and said you would hunt them down if they didn't let her go."

A wry smile raised a corner of Nathan's mouth. "That sounds like the Baylee I know. What else?"

"The man said and I quote, 'Your boyfriend and his Navy SEAL friends will think twice about disrupting our organization's activities after I'm finished with you.'"

"You must have heard the conversation right. That matches the content of the note delivered to me earlier." Nathan's face flushed and he mopped sweat from his brow with the back of his hand, his body language showing nearly a break down level of stress. "I never should have left her alone."

Clearly, Nathan adored Baylee. The guy struck her as the tough-guy type that hid his emotions, but today distress was written all over his face. She felt compelled to ease his suffering. "It's not your fault. Those men were obviously hell bent on getting to her. And apparently you know why. Right now we need to focus on finding her."

"That's easy to say, but we have no clue where he's taken her."

"What's going on here?" Karl asked.

Oh, shit, no. Jamie's neck and shoulder muscles tightened while her nerve endings jumped to life.

"Baylee's been kidnapped." Nathan spoke in a rumbling, angry voice. "The Muslim Alliance took her and plans to kill her as a revenge move against our recent activities."

"How do you know they were responsible?" Karl's voice sounded severe and mission oriented, not at all like the voice Jamie remembered when they were nestled in each other's arms, stroking each other, gazing into each other's eyes.

Jamie gritted her teeth and willed herself to focus.

"A mysterious man delivered a letter to me at the pool. It seems that Jamie overheard the actual kidnapping."

"Seriously? And she didn't call hotel security in time to stop it?" Karl's voice burned with irritation.

Anger simmered to the surface hearing him speak about her as if she weren't even in the room. Feeling Karl's hot gaze on her back, she swung around to face him, determined to vent her frustration. She opened her mouth to speak, but stopped when Nathan jumped in to defend her.

"There's nothing she could have done to stop this. These men were probably heavily armed," said Nathan. "And she was asleep when all this was happening."

"Asleep? I don't get it." Karl's ocean blue eyes had transformed to a stormy gray and his thick dark brows had drawn together.

His harsh expression disarmed her, making her forget the angry retort she'd been about to launch his way. He looked at her like she was a guilty criminal not a woman he'd once been in love with. *It's over for us. Why can't you stop imagining otherwise?* "I—I'm not sure I heard it right," she stammered.

"I was asleep and I think because of all the noise, Baylee's kidnapping entered my dream. That's why I didn't do anything. Wait, what I mean is that I would have done something to help if I could have for sure, but during the nightmare, I couldn't move a muscle. It was like my whole body was paralyzed.

"I tried to run, to shout out, but I couldn't. And I didn't know my nightmare was really happening until I woke up." *Wow, that came out making zero sense.* Jamie clamped her lips together as her face flushed hot.

The corners of Karl's usually sexy mouth turned up in a sneer. "Why don't you leave this to the police and the other people trained for this type of work? They should be able to come up with some solid evidence. You're only making this worse for Nathan. You've got him worked up into knots over this dream nonsense."

Jamie ground her teeth together until her jaw muscles cramped. She was so angry, her mind momentarily blocked out the attraction, hurt and confusion that warred in her mind long enough to lash out at him in full force.

She leaned in toward him, raised her voice and slammed a finger into his chest. "You're an intelligent man so I'm sure you heard Nathan say the note he found threatened her life. I didn't say anything he didn't already know."

"Why are you being so hard on her? She's your girlfriend, remember?"

"She is *not* my girlfriend." Karl's tone was laced with malice.

Jamie choked on her next breath. The words stung way worse than they should have.

Nathan threw a harsh look at Karl and then an almost apologetic one in Jamie's direction. "What's gotten into you, man? Stop hassling her. If Jamie overheard the actual conversation, that's important stuff and I want to hear it."

Karl shook his head, clearly unconvinced. "I don't see how hearing about her dream will help us find Baylee."

By now, Jamie was seething. "Damn it, Karl. Will you stop talking about me as if I'm not in the room?"

"We were getting somewhere before you showed up, Patterson," Nathan said in an angry voice. "Will you shut up and let her talk?"

"Fine, let's hear her story." The sarcastic way he said the word story was impossible not to notice.

Jamie rolled her eyes at him before speaking. *What did I ever see in him? He's acting like such a prick.* "Right, my story. Which I'm only telling, by the way, because I want to help." She perched her hands on her hips. There would be no more cowering in front of her ex. She was sick and tired of his arrogant behavior. "I think after they kidnapped her, they took her to another hotel. The men mentioned the *Ionian Gypsy*."

Officer Laskaris was crouched on the floor examining pieces of the splintered chair. He pushed himself to his feet and met her gaze. "That's not a hotel. That's an older cruising boat owned by a local tour operator. He takes groups of triathletes and other aquatically inclined tourists out for ocean swims along several nearby islands."

Jamie didn't try to hide her smug smile when Karl's eyes widened with interest.

"I'll be damned," Nathan said. "This lady's got a head on her shoulders." After giving a nod of approval to Jamie, he wrinkled his brow and glanced in Karl's direction. "We'd be looking for her by now if dickhead here hadn't delayed us with all his flack."

Jamie nearly burst out laughing when Karl shifted uneasily on his feet and shrugged. *Guess the cat got his tongue.*

The police officer glanced at his watch. "The swimmers usually go to Kalamos and Kastos Islands on Tuesdays, but they should be returning to the dock any minute."

"Let's go check it out," said Nathan. "We're planning to meet a group of Delta Force guys and FBI agents down there anyway."

CHAPTER TEN

May 25, 2016
Nikiana Hotel
Lefkada Island, Greece
1535 hours

Jamie shielded her eyes from the blinding sunlight as she exited the building and followed the group of on-a-mission men. Karl had passed her in the hallway without saying a word and now walked just ahead of her on the winding pathway leading down to the beach. An olive tree branch scratched at her arm and she shoved it away with frustration. *He could have at least apologized.*

Vowing to remain angry with him, she struggled to unglue her eyes from his athletic hamstring and calf muscles that flexed as his feet negotiated the rugged sand and rock pathway. She moistened her lips with her tongue, distracted by how his muscular buttocks filled out his khaki shorts. *Reflecting on Karl's hotness won't get me anywhere. Thinking how rude and arrogant he acted a minute ago would be much more worthwhile.*

As much as she fought it, her thoughts bounced back to the past. Their meeting in Paris had been like a scene straight from a movie. Her hair singed, her lungs choking on noxious smoke, she'd been about to perish in a hotel fire. He'd appeared out of the inferno, scooping her up in his arms and carrying her to safety.

For an instant she'd forgotten the roar of the flames and the searing pain of flame on tender flesh. For that tiny snapshot of time, all that had existed were Karl's masculine features in front of her face—the olive complexion, the sculpted jaw line, the mesmerizing blue eyes flecked with silver and aquamarine. Safe was how she'd felt with this powerful, competent, and strong man.

When he'd held her against his fortress-like body and carried her from the burning hotel, her body had hummed with excitement over the physical contact. Sure, she'd been terrified and physically spent, but the undercurrent of sexual excitement had reminded her that she still breathed, that her heart was still beating, that she was human. She'd clung to every message her senses delivered to her eyes, her ears, her nerve endings, feeling grateful to be alive. She'd wanted to witness tomorrow's sunrise, to ask her rescuer if he felt as much attraction toward her as she did toward him.

She gritted her teeth and released a long sigh. *Stop this, Jamie. He was your hero then, but today he's just another arrogant jerk.* The surly interchange hurt more than she cared to admit. Karl had always struck her as considerate and gentlemanly. Any time he'd expressed annoyance or anger toward her in past instances had been out of fear for her safety.

She had been more than a little bull-headed after he'd rescued her in Paris. She'd been in a hospital bed watching the news when she saw him and others from his team rush into Charles de Gaulle airport.

Without waiting to be released, she'd rushed straight to the scene despite the threat of a terrorist attack. She'd even refused to leave when the threat of chemical warfare had become imminent and a gunman launched an attack.

Today, she'd done nothing to earn the cold treatment she'd received. Not only had he shown no regards for her feelings, he'd spoken to her like she didn't have a working brain cell between her ears.

Maybe I don't know him as well as I thought I did. This hardened and uncaring side of him she'd seen earlier was the antipode of the Karl she'd fallen in love with, that she'd fantasized about spending the rest of her life with.

Maybe he's changed. He'd always kept details of his Navy SEAL missions under wraps. She understood the reasoning behind his silence, but still...Sometimes her curious mind had gone crazy envisioning scenarios of his top-secret operations. She'd wanted so badly to know about the happenings she wasn't privy to.

She'd read enough memoirs written by Navy SEALs and Deltas to convince her that too much death and destruction could change a person. Or even destroy them.

I wonder how many people he's killed? A few, dozens, hundreds? She had no way of knowing. Most missions involved raiding buildings where multiple targets were taken out. Sure, their targets were terrorists or people hell bent on destruction and mayhem, but they were still human beings. Maybe for a while he cringed at those up-close views of blood and brains spattered against walls. And then something changed.

How many times could you see someone's head blown off before your heart turned to stone? There had to be a threshold and maybe Karl had exceeded it. His hardened heart wouldn't notice a wounded facial expression or empathize with bruised feelings.

Distracted by her unwieldy thoughts, Jamie stumbled over a rock. It happened too quickly for her to regain her balance. Her head jerked back from the impact as her hands and knees struck the uneven ground. "Ouch," she cried.

Karl stopped walking and turned to face her. Instead of the gunmetal cold she had expected, sea blue eyes gazed at her wide with concern. "Are you okay?" He strode toward her, crouched down and reached for her hand.

Jamie's hands and knees burned from the hard landing. She studied her palm to find it was scraped and bleeding. Her unruly, not-quite-dry hair curtained her eyes.

She tossed the rogue lock aside and looked up at Karl's proffered hand—so large and sturdy and strong—and into the face she'd once loved. She recognized those eyes. Right now they studied her the same way they always had since the very first day they'd met. She forced her eyes into a sustained blink, hoping when she opened them again, her reason would return.

Don't fall for it. He isn't the same. "I'm fine. It's just a little scratch." Instead of taking his hand, she ground her molars together so she could tolerate the pain that shot through one knee as she made a shaky ascent to standing. "We should get going. We're falling behind."

The others had already reached the beach. Families with children and couples frolicked in the water. Dozens of other people lounged on chaises shielded from the sun by large blue umbrellas. One small fishing boat was docked alongside the small concrete docking area. Four other boats had anchored offshore and people were swimming around the boats, savoring a dip in the inviting water that was aquamarine in the shallow area near the shore and transformed to a brilliant, deep blue further out.

Karl's hand closed around her arm, firm and strong. "You're hurt. There are enough men on this case to handle the situation. Why don't you let me take you back to the hotel? I'll get you bandaged up and comfortable so you can rest."

His grip on her bare arm warmed her skin with more intensity than the late afternoon sun. This wasn't sun-on-body heat. Sun-on-body heat warmed only the surface of the skin and was soothing, comforting, sleep-inducing. This was a sensual heat that tantalized every molecule from the surface of her skin to the depth of her bones.

This heat jerked her into a state of high-alertness where it felt amazing to be alive and tragic at the same time because what her body craved felt so far out of reach. She longed to touch him. Again and again and again.

She heard a man shout and snapped her gaze toward what was happening on the beach. More than a dozen men had jumped off an inflatable boat after driving it up onto the sand. People had jumped up from their chairs and approached to ask what was happening. Officer Laskaris stood a few feet away like a barricade, addressing the curious tourists in a harsh tone of voice.

After speaking loud and fast in Greek, he broke into English, telling everyone to stay back and that there was no cause for alarm.

The reinforcements are here so they don't need me to help find Baylee. She was tempted to give in, to take Karl's hand and see where that led them. No. I can't. *I'll regret it later.* Fighting against the attraction she felt, Jamie spoke in a surlier tone than she intended. "I already told you I'm fine. I don't need you to watch out for me."

"Okay. I was just worried, that's all." Frowning, he released her arm and crossed his arms in front of this chest.

She didn't want to notice his drawn-together brows, the hurt flicker in the depth of his blue eyes. *His feelings aren't my problem anymore.* Her body and heart argued against that concept. She cared about him every bit as much as she wanted him to care about her. *Why? What is the matter with me?* "Right. You were worried about me. That's why you penned me for an idiot in front of everyone back there."

An apology appeared in his expression before it was spoken. "I'm sorry. What I said came out all wrong. I was just worried about Nathan, that's all. The poor guy's a wreck."

Jamie didn't want to accept his apology, she wanted to lash out and release her pent up pain. "It's no problem," she said in a sarcastic tenor. "You did the right thing. It's much more important to consider the feelings of longtime friends than a woman you had a short-term affair with and have already forgotten."

She perched her hands on her hips and swiped at a lock of hair the sea breeze had blown in her face. "As a matter of fact, I'm surprised you didn't bring your new girlfriend on this outing."

Jamie brushed against his shoulder as she pushed past him and walked with a huffy stride toward the beach. His running footsteps thundered on the hard ground behind her. She increased her pace, trying to stay ahead of him, but the trail was steep and rugged and she couldn't move any faster without falling on her face again.

"Girlfriend? What g—" Karl's hot breath blew into her ear.

"I don't want to talk about it." A titillating tingle lingered on Jamie's neck, but she forced herself not to dwell on it. The trail came to an abrupt end on the white sand beach. Her feet sunk deep into the sand as she strode far enough down the beach to better see what was happening without catching the attention of the police officer. She jerked to a stop and crossed her arms in front of her chest.

While his companion fended off the gathering spectators, Officer Laskaris strode toward an empty mooring space and pointed toward an approaching boat.

"That's the swim tour boat," said Laskaris, speaking to plain clothed, armed men gathered around him. "When the *Ionian Gypsy* docks, I'll order the swimmers and crew to disembark without delay so we can board and do a search." He directed his gaze toward Nathan and Darryl. "It would be best if you two waited here."

Jamie could tell the way Nathan threw his hands in the air that he had no intention of complying with the suggestion.

"Screw that. I've been trained to deal with situations like this. I have to know if Baylee's on board that boat." Instead of making the requested retreat, Nathan stepped closer to the edge of the dock and defiantly crossed his arms over his chest.

By now the *Ionian Gypsy* was idling and gliding in toward the dock.

"I know you told me earlier you were special ops guys, but your personal involvement complicated things," said Laskaris. "And I haven't had time to confirm your identities."

A muscle bound man with a buzz cut who Jamie guessed might be a Delta opened his mouth to speak, but Darryl spoke before he had a chance to say anything.

"The Delta Force guys know about us. We intend to let you guys do your jobs and stay in the background."

Officer Laskaris directed a stern gaze toward the Delta, waiting for his response.

The Delta wiped his brow and flicked his large hand to release wet drops of sweat into the sand. "Officer Laskaris, we've confirmed their IDs. One of their superiors was our initial contact. They can stay for now. Not that I'm welcoming the company. Bringing along rogue dudes emotionally attached to the victim isn't our normal modus operandi."

Darryl's taut facial features and commanding voice showed he wasn't pleased with what had been said. "Now wait. This isn't a question of emotional involvement. We're the target here and we know how this enemy operates. We should be involved in this pursuit."

Jamie laced her hands behind her back, watching the macho man contest play out. After more heated debate, the men came to an agreement. The Delta Force leader spoke to a man who had jumped from the bow and was securing the *Ionian Gypsy* with rope to metal cleats on the dock.

The weathered sailing yacht had a varnished wooden hull and cabin and was at least 50 feet long. With its size, Jamie figured it probably hosted some below deck rooms. Perhaps Nathan's girlfriend had been bound, gagged and locked away without the tourists even knowing she were aboard.

Had Baylee heard voices while the swimmers were on board and squirmed, wishing desperately someone would find her? *God, how awful.* She wanted to see a happy ending to this nightmare—Baylee alive and well and back in Nathan's arms where she belonged. Instead, she had to turn her back on the situation and hope it turned out okay.

"Come on, let's get out of here." Karl's hand brushed over one of her shoulders before coming to rest on her upper back. He gave her a gentle push to turn her toward the hotel.

Jamie knew lingering on the beach wouldn't help get Baylee back, but she sure as hell didn't want to take orders from Karl. Refusing to budge, she jutted one hip in his direction. "You have no say in my life or what I do anymore. Why don't you get that?"

Karl took a step back and scratched at his forehead with a sweaty hand. "What is this about? I understand you're upset over what I said earlier, but I said I'm sorry. And what is all this talk about me having a girlfriend?"

More fury surged up as she studied his stymied expression. Damn sexy was how that crinkled brow and asymmetrical frown made him look, as much as she hated to admit it. A muscle in his cheek twitched.

"The brunette you were flirting with in the lobby earlier, who do you think?" She cringed when she heard the jealous ring to her voice instead of the I don't give a shit nonchalance she'd planned on projecting.

Karl's surprised expression melted away and a laugh escaped his lips. "Wait. I can explain."

So glad he finds this funny. I on the other hand, would like to serve him up a roundhouse punch straight to the side of his thick head. "I'm sure you can."

He'd always seemed genuine and humble whenever he'd spoken to her in the past. He'd always been willing to discuss any topic that was on her mind and had done his best to ease her worries when they were first getting to know each other.

That was then. He's different now. Jamie took a step and pushed past him, intending to make a break for the hotel.

"Jamie, stop. Why won't you listen? The woman you're needlessly worrying about is Olivia."

Jamie jerked to a stop and turned to face him as an embarrassed flush warmed her face and chest. *This is super awkward.* "Olivia?" Her voice came out in a whisper.

"Yes, Olivia. Darryl's bride-to-be. I've known her for two years. We're on friendly terms, but certainly not the way you're thinking." Karl drew a hand to his wrinkled brow, wiping away sweat. "You were jealous when you saw me talking to her. That's why you stormed off. Why, Jamie? As I recall, you dumped me. If I wasn't the man you wanted, why shouldn't I seek companionship with someone else?"

Distress was written all over his face. The shallow water green tones in his eyes overpowered the rich blue ones, the same way they had in Paris when she'd expressed concerns he might be putting up a gentlemanly front and not really wanting to follow through with their impending affair.

Looking at that mouth of his—that made her breath catch in her throat in any configuration—was a dead giveaway he was upset. She felt compelled to kiss those full lips even if they were turned down in a frown. She released a long sigh and hung her head. *How could I have misread this situation so badly?* "There's no reason you shouldn't date someone else, I guess."

She couldn't stop herself from appending her ambivalence to her sentence. Him with another woman wasn't something she wanted to envision.

What a mess. Nothing about the day had gone as expected. It had started with lost luggage and had escalated to kidnapping and a close and very uncomfortable encounter with her ex-boyfriend that she now knew she still loved.

"God, this can't be happening," she muttered, unable to restrain her frustration with her unwieldy emotions and the situation. She turned and started to walk slowly up the beach, sensing he was following her even after she'd started up the path leading toward the hotel. Karl's touch on her shoulder brought her to an abrupt halt and she turned to face him.

He pulled his hand from her shoulder and dropped it heavily to his side. "Can you stop speaking in ambiguities and tell me what's going on here?" He spoke in that familiar southern accent she'd always been drawn to. There was a strain of frustration around the edges of every word, but they were spoken slowly enough for her to know he was willing to hear her out.

She recalled what an attentive listener he'd been over the course of their time together. He'd even listened with a compassionate ear to her distress over body image anxieties that lingered following a relationship with an overly critical boyfriend.

Karl had never responded with half-hearted *uh huh*s and *I see*s. His gaze had been riveted on her face whenever she'd spoken and his responses had indicated that he'd heard her and was trying to understand what she was feeling.

If I can calm down and talk to him like I did before all this crap happened I'll know for sure if he's changed or if I'm imagining things. Whether it sounded lame or not, she was going to lay her feelings on the table. "I'm beyond overwhelmed."

She dumped out her frustration over her travel experiences and how she'd deliberated for days over attending the wedding. She recognized empathy in his eyes. She wondered if he, too, had studied the wedding invitation and wanted to attend but had fretted over how he would handle running into Jamie. The understanding she saw in his expression gave her the courage to express what was foremost in her mind. "The jealousy wasn't something I expected, it just happened. Seeing you talking to another woman..." Her voice broke.

"Jamie, I don't understand. I thought you wanted me out of your life."

"I didn't really. And now I'm more confused than ever. On one hand I feel like I made a mistake about us and wish I could take it back. I only did it because I thought our relationship was becoming a burden to you."

Karl shook his head and gave her a flummoxed expression. "A burden to me. How could you ever think that?"

"It's not your fault. I guess it was my own insecurity that led me to call it off. We didn't seem to be on the same wavelength after so much time apart."

"I know." Karl's voice was somber and hollow sounding.

"When I saw you again, all the memories rushed back." She sighed. "I don't even know how to express what I was feeling. But when you attacked me earlier, I thought maybe our breakup wasn't a mistake, that maybe you'd changed and you weren't the same Karl I met in Paris and fell in love with."

"We all change. Life has a way of doing that to us." The look on his face looked almost tragic. The sorrow she saw in the depth of his eyes suggested he'd suffered a major loss. Was it possible that loss had anything to do with her?

"How have you changed? Was it something that happened on one of your missions?"

"No. It happened after you broke my heart when I was going t—" He paused. "Oh, well, it's over and done with."

Jamie was too stunned to speak. He was telling her the incident that had changed him forever wasn't a falling body, a downed comrade, a blown off head, it was something she'd said.

She wondered what he'd planned to say and had restrained from telling her that night she'd suggested they date others. Maybe he had been granted a couple days leave and had wanted to spend that time together. Did it even matter what he'd planned to say now that so many months had passed? "I suppose it is. I know I can't take it back." Tears filled her eyes. Feeling embarrassed, she looked away.

"Don't be so sure about that." Karl's voice was gentle and compassionate. He stepped in close enough that his masculine scent and nearness scattered her thoughts.

"W-what did you say?" She had to be sure she'd heard him right. *Is he opening the door for us to try again? Why do I care? This can't work.*

"Jamie, please. I'm not going to pry the words out of your mouth." Karl cleared his throat and kicked a toe into the bone-dry earth.

It made sense that he wanted her to voice her feelings before he opened himself up to being burned again. Still, she didn't want to burst out with the first thoughts that popped into her head. She had to do this right. She had to convince him she still cared for him, that she had ended things because it had seemed better for both of them at the time. And if he shared her desire to be together again...

Her thoughts drifted off into fantasy, imagining them together again and for the first time since arriving in Greece, she allowed her senses to immerse themselves in the idyllic surroundings.

The hot late afternoon sun was a sensuous touch on her bare shoulders, the sea breeze a feathery tickle. And the Ionian Sea. No photograph or painting could capture that rich, vibrant gemstone quality cerulean blue. Jamie wanted to form a mental picture of that breathtaking stretch of sea in her mind so she would remember it forever.

The tension in her neck and shoulders subsided as she drew the salty sea air deep into her lungs. *I feel like myself again.* The out-of-synch feeling she had experienced after their break-up had been one reason she had pushed herself so hard in recent months. Staying in constant motion was safe, while slowing her pace allowed too much time for self-reflection and longing for Karl.

She hadn't even noticed how out-of-touch she had become with herself until she'd boarded the plane for Athens. Out of her comfort zone didn't even describe how she'd felt the past twelve hours. Jamie had never needed a relationship to be whole. She'd spent most of her adult life single and self-sufficient. But after she'd ended it with Karl, she'd been so afraid to mourn the loss of her relationship that she'd avoided activities that kept her life balanced and buried herself in work.

Instead of awakening early each morning to linger over the morning paper and sip her coffee, she had swallowed her coffee on the bus to work while responding to emails on her smart phone.

Instead of strolling in Luxembourg Park on evenings and weekends, she had tackled extra projects and parked herself in front of her laptop, staying too busy to think. I'm a writer she'd told herself over and over to justify her ridiculous schedule. On the plane, she'd felt vulnerable without a computer screen to hide behind. *Rushing around in an oblivious stupor isn't living. How could I have done this to myself?*

I was so worried that he'd changed, when I'm the one who has changed for the worse. Is it even fair to ask for a second chance?

Jamie sighed. She hadn't exactly had her shit totally together when they'd met. In those days, her inability to overcome guilt over her brother's injury in a fire that had consumed their family home years ago had kept her from setting challenging career goals. She'd overcome that obstacle only to transform into a workaholic. *Everyone has issues. Why don't you figure out what he wants and go from there.* "I'm sorry I'm taking so long to answer. I just want to say this right."

"I'm not in any hurry," Karl said gently.

Her vibrant and alive personality that had been stilted for so long ached to burst out and shout *I'm free*. He'd indicated there was a chance of reconciliation.

She clung to that hope as she studied his face, hoping he'd welcome her back in his life. But things would be different from now on, regardless of his response. *I want my life back.*

Even if he said they were over and done with, she wouldn't go back to living the way she had for the past several months. She'd grieve and get over him and move on to build a real and meaningful life. *I want to take an hour to drink a cup of coffee, sprawl out on a soft green lawn and watch a sunset. And sprawl out in one of those lounge chairs on this amazing beach and read a book or sit in the sand by the water and feel a cool wave curl over my feet.*

In the back of her mind, she kept thinking all of those experiences would be so much more colorful with Karl in her life. *Should I pour out an apology? Belabor the point that we were drifting apart? Or say I was confused? Tell him I'm in shabby shape to be in a relationship?* Her mind was in turmoil. She couldn't predict his moods and reactions anymore. She met his gaze, wondering if he noticed how her hands trembled, if he saw flickers of worry in her eyes.

"What are you afraid of?"

"I don't know. I've made a mess of my life lately."

"I don't think so. You're a talented broadcast journalist with an inquisitive mind and a beautiful woman who lives in Paris, a city most people would kill to even visit. Many women would love to have your life.

"You seem to take it and yourself for granted. Cut yourself a break, Jamie, instead of being hard on yourself. You said a minute ago you couldn't take it back. What did you mean by that?" His deep, southern accented voice soothed her ears. A calm blue had replaced the stormy turbulence she'd seen in his eyes moments ago.

Jamie opened her mouth to answer him, but paused when she saw a group of eight tourists walking up the path. She wrung her hands and sighed, stepping off the trail beside Karl to make room for them to pass.

A tall and lanky high school aged boy with sun-bleached hair and a large red waterproof duffel slung over his shoulder was the first one to walk by them. He looks like a swimmer, Jamie thought. She could picture him wearing sleek goggles over his eyes and puffing out a last breath as he stepped up on the blocks for a race.

Everyone in the group had a white dusting of dried seawater on their sun-bronzed skin and wet hair. Most of the women wore brightly colored sarongs over bikinis or colorful one-piece suits.

The stragglers in the group were two women engrossed in conversation; one tan and freckled, the other with soft skin white as snow. The fair skinned woman spoke in a British accent and wore khaki shorts, a royal blue swimsuit and a tan hat to shield her face from the sun. The tanned, muscular woman spoke in a distinctly Midwestern accent. A colorful sarong cocooned her body and large dark sunglasses and a bright red hat obscured most of her face. "Those swims today were amazing. I've never seen so many dolphins." A breeze lifted a corner of the American woman's sarong, revealing part of her orange and red swimsuit.

"Neither have I." The British woman jerked to a stop, reached into her backpack for a blue rash guard and pulled it over her head to cover her sun-reddened shoulders, and then resumed her leisurely walking pace. "It seemed like they wanted to play with us, the way they dove down deep and then spiraled up right near us. This swimming holiday has been lovely even though this day turned out quite odd."

Jamie wondered what she meant about the day being odd. Why hadn't the Deltas and the FBI agents queried these people before searching the boat? Maybe they knew what had happened to Baylee.

The women greeted Jamie and Karl with a friendly *hello*.

Jamie returned the greeting and then decided to take the initiative and engage them in conversation to see if she could uncover any useful information. "I overheard you talking about swimming in the ocean," said Jamie. "Are you with that swimming vacation tour group?"

"We are. I'm Christine," said the blonde-haired British woman. "And my new friend here is Lisa."

Jamie turned to greet the compact woman with the lean, muscular physique who looked like she never missed a swimming workout. "Nice to meet you. I'm Jamie and this is my...friend Karl. The sea is so clear and beautiful; swimming out there must have been an amazing experience. I don't swim often, but I'd certainly enjoy it here."

"I'm sure Kallistos would let you join us one day if you wanted to," said Lisa. "Two people cancelled at the last minute so there's plenty of room on the boat for more."

If she and Karl didn't resolve things, the swim might be just the distraction she needed. And if they did work things out, maybe he'd want to go with her. He was a strong swimmer and the water was such a lovely aquamarine color in the shallow areas and so crystal clear. They probably would swim along remote places on these islands where...*Keep your head in the conversation, will you?* "I might take you up on that."

"You wouldn't want to miss it." Christine raved about their day of swimming around islands where they saw colorful fish, dolphins and bunched up layers of limestone and poked their heads into caves. While the two women *oohed* and *aahed* over their experience, Jamie politely nodded. She redirected her thoughts away from images of her and Karl swimming side by side through the clear water to gleaning information.

"You were on the *Ionian Gypsy*, right?"

Christine burst out with, "Yeah, that's our boat. I don't understand why people are so bloody interested in it. She's a bit of a relic, sixty or so years old, Kallistos told us, but really. The minute we reached the dock, these blokes who looked like special investigators ordered us to disembark straight away. We barely had time to gather our things."

After removing her sunglasses, Lisa pushed the brim of her hat away from her eyes and met Jamie's gaze. "They said they planned to do a search. They sounded so serious, like they expected to find drugs onboard or something."

"A friend of ours was kidnapped and those men suspect she might have been taken aboard," said Jamie.

"Kidnapped? No way," Lisa's dark brown eyes opened wider.

"Yes, the missing woman's name is Baylee Stiles and she was taken from her hotel room."

Christine directed her gaze back toward the brilliant blue sea and the moored boat that was now swarming with men. "That's terrible. Lefkada seems so quiet and safe, but I've had this dreadful feeling something wasn't right."

Lisa tapped the side of her face with her folded up sunglasses and frowned. "Me, too. This afternoon's trip was really sketchy."

Jamie's journalistic personality clicked into gear. She wanted to know the how, when, what and why. "Tell us every detail about your afternoon. Especially anything that seemed suspicious or might give us a clue about what happened to Baylee."

"Sure, I'd be delighted to help," said Christine.

Lisa nodded and said, "Yes, me, too. What happened is so terrible. It would be great if we could help you find your friend."

The two women looked at each other and shrugged. Lisa bit her lip and Christine tapped a sandaled foot into the sand before speaking. "I'm not sure what information would be useful to you, though."

"How about if I ask a few questions and then if any other details that seem important pop into your head, you just go ahead and share those as well?"

The two women nodded in response. Their anxiety seemingly forgotten, they both looked at her with unblinking, focused gazes.

"Where did your guides take you today?"

"We went to Meganisi, Kithros, Kalamos, and Kastos Island," said Christine.

"Wow. That sounds like a lot of swimming," said Jamie.

"We swim nearly five kilometers each day," said Lisa. "But it doesn't seem difficult because the seawater is so buoyant and there is so much to see underwater and around the islands."

"Despite the distance, our swims aren't all work," Christine added. "This morning we snorkeled around in Papanikolis Cave just looking at rock formations and fish. It's really ama—"

"Wait, let's get back to what you both said earlier—about this afternoon's tour being sketchy and odd. What did you mean by that?"

Lisa's dark brown eyes widened as if she were preparing to say something important. "The first clue that something was off was when the guides brought us back to Nikiana for lunch. Our itinerary said we would eat lunch in a small village on Kalamos Island. We were starved and it took forever to get all the way back here."

"Did the guides explain why your plans changed?"

Christine nodded. "Kallistos said the boat required a bit of repair and that he needed to return to Nikiana for parts. He said while he and Alexios serviced the boat, we were to dine at the hotel. He seemed unbelievably anxious. He must have glanced at his watch dozens of times and he kept cracking his knuckles, which I'd never seen him do before. Usually, he seemed quite relaxed, really."

"Did you overhear either of the men making phone calls or anything else that seemed strange?" Jamie asked.

"Kallistos phoned a couple of times. He raised his voice and sounded quite angry, really. After docking the boat, he and Alexios helped us off the boat and then dashed off like their arses were on fire," said Christine. "It was bloody strange. Two men so relaxed they could nod off in the middle of a conversation suddenly so bloody hexed about a simple boat repair."

"What happened after that?"

"After lunch and a cup of tea, we returned to the dock at the designated meeting time. We waited more than thirty minutes before two beastly looking blokes we'd never seen before showed up saying they were leading the afternoon swim since Kallistos and his brother had decided to take the afternoon off. Before we got on board, they loaded quite a lot of stuff on the boat."

"Can you give us a basic description of the two men?" Karl asked

"Stephanos had a hairy gorilla chest," said Lisa.

Christine burst out laughing. "Yeah, he was a primate of the first order. I know that sounds catty. But he was a dreadful mean bloke. He bit our heads off about almost everything and treated us like we were a bloody nuisance."

"Did either man have any other distinguishing features?"

"I did see that Stephanos and the other guy Titos both had knife tattoos on their arms," said Lisa.

"Did they carry anything on board large enough to hide a person?" Jamie asked.

Christine waved a hand through the air as if to emphasize her answer. "Yes, and that was odd, too. When I offered to help load things, that nasty excuse for a man snapped at me and told me to mind my own business. He and Titos carried this large cylindrical container onboard that looked like a water storage tank.

"Their cheeks were puffing out like blowfish they were straining so hard to carry it despite the fact that they have biceps two times the size of my thighs. It probably would have held a few hundred gallons full.

"That thing would have been way too heavy for any bloke to carry filled with water and empty it would have been a paperweight for those two. They stowed it below decks in the galley where we had been warned to stay out by Kallistos since they were still fixing it up.

He'd said there might be protruding nails or other hazards down there."

Jamie's voice rang with excitement. "Maybe they brought Baylee onboard inside that container."

Lisa's mouth twisted into a frustrated frown. "Damn it, I wished we'd known something was wrong. We assumed Kallistos was sick or had a family emergency and was trying not to alarm us."

"There's no way you could have known a situation like this was brewing." Jamie opened her mouth to ask another question, but then paused when she heard Karl's voice.

"Did they continue to act suspicious after that?" Karl asked.

Both women nodded, their eyes wide with affirmation.

"Yes, they did. Both of them seemed distracted and continued to bark at us all afternoon," said Lisa. She tightened the knot on her colorful wrap that hugged one shoulder and was starting to slip loose. "Stephanos didn't do a thing to help Tyler when he got stung by a jellyfish and abandoned us during most of our swim."

Jamie didn't know much about open water swimming and must have looked mystified because Lisa quickly jumped in with a more detailed explanation.

"Usually the boat stays alongside us throughout the swim so they can give us water and drinks, protect us from passing boats and make sure no one is in trouble. This time they dropped us at the starting point of our swim and then left us so we crossed that rough channel from Kalamos to Kastos unescorted, even though it was really choppy and someone could have gotten into trouble," Lisa added.

"Since we know each others' abilities fairly well, we teamed up in twos and watched out for each other and looked around for approaching boats. The *Ionian Gypsy* reappeared only after we had swum more than a kilometer around the rim of Kastos Island and we were swimming toward the beach where we'd planned to end the swim.

"Stephanos acted like leaving us out there was perfectly normal and even though we were all dehydrated after that long swim, he didn't offer us any water, chocolate or snacks. When we asked for him to throw us the bottles, he said we could get on the boat and get them ourselves."

"I know, right? The bloke's a bloody piece of work."

"A complete jerk if you ask me," added Lisa.

"Do you think Baylee's still on the boat?" Jamie asked.

"I would wager she's not," said Christine. "I imagine they dropped her somewhere during that time they left us swimming the channel alone."

"That would make sense."

"Also, while we were lounging about, catching our breath on Kastos Island, I noticed that ugly gray water tank they'd stowed on board had been stashed in the sand. When I asked Stephanos about it, he gave me a surly response about it being an emergency water supply in case anyone ran out of water. When Mike said he needed to refill his water bottle and began to walk toward it, Stephanos screamed at him to fill it with the jug on the boat. The man was a loon."

"He certainly sounds like it. Did anything else out of the ordinary happen?" Jamie asked.

"Yeah, one more thing," said Christine. "After the swim to Kastos Island, the boat stopped at Kathisma, another town on this island a distance away from our original landing spot.

"Both men disembarked, spoke in Greek to some men at the dock and said a different driver would take us back to Lefkada Town. I saw Stephanos hand the man a wad of cash and then he and the other guy rushed off in a hurry. It was a dreadful trip back here. Our regular captain, Alexios, was a master seaman. He's got bloody big muscles, wears a serious, stern expression and is tanned to the color of leather.

" When I try to jest with him, he looks at me like he thinks I'm a loon, but that man knows how to read the waves. The bloke they left us with wasn't skilled at all in handling the boat in rough waters. We were tossed all over the place and the boat took in a lot of water. Some of us were so scared we were hanging onto the life buoys in case we tipped over."

"That sounds like a terrible experience," said Jamie.

"It wasn't all that bad, really. We're all strong swimmers and we were never all that far from an island," said Lisa. "I figured if he sunk the boat, we could swim for it."

"You're braver than I would have been." Jamie glanced down toward the beach, wondering if the search party had uncovered anything during their search. "We need to have you tell all this to Officers Laskaris and Kara-something-or other...I can't quite remember that younger policeman's name, but you'll know him when you see him." She blushed and glanced away when Karl gave her a stern, questioning look. "By the uniform," she added hastily.

"Do you mind accompanying us so you can explain what you've told us?" Karl asked.

"No, not at all," the two women said at once.

"I'd wager those men abandoned Baylee on Kastos Island and intend to let her die of exposure," said Jamie.

"That's terrible. Its so hot today." Lisa opened her mouth to say more but seemed to decide it was better not to.

She was probably going to say she could be dead by now. "Do you think you could identify your landing spot on Kastos Island from a boat?"

"Yeah, I think so. The islands all have unique shapes and I remember what the beach and the coast around it looked like," said Christine.

"So much of it looked the same. I carried my waterproof camera on the swim. I took a bunch of photos of the coast. Maybe we can use those to figure out exactly where we landed," said Lisa.

"The policemen and the others will probably want to look through the images during the trip out there," said Jamie. "But right now we need to get going. Baylee's life is in grave danger and we've got no time to lose."

CHAPTER ELEVEN

May 25, 2016
Kastos Island, Greece
1545 hours

Baylee drifted in and out of consciousness, feeling as though her brain were melting as the all-encompassing heat suffocated her. Her skin and clothing, drenched with sweat, clung to the bottom of the plastic water storage tank where she lay inside trapped.

Two muscle bound men wearing tank tops and scary tattoos had stealthily entered her hotel room. She'd kicked, punched and screamed, but to no avail. In an instant, the larger of the men she now knew was Stephanos had snapped her hands behind her back and bound them. After gagging her, they'd dragged her down the hall and stairway.

Outside the building, they'd forced motion sickness tablets down her throat before shoving her down the path leading to the beach. They led her to a grove of olive trees where they'd stashed a large water storage tank. They had been just steps away from the beach where dozens of tourists were milling about. She'd desperately wished one of them would notice the flash of movement in the trees.

Even if someone happened to be looking their way, they probably wouldn't have suspected anything life threatening were happening. The observer might have imagined someone stopped to take a leak or a couple was stealing a kiss or a quick fuck and gone back to spreading another layer of sunscreen over his or her body. She hadn't had much choice other than to comply when Stephanos held a gun to her temple and joked about spilling her brains all over the concrete dock.

She'd taken one last look at the sunlight dancing across the blue green water before climbing into the storage tank she feared would soon become her coffin. Part of her had already died the moment she'd capitulated. It wasn't like her to agree to terms that didn't suit her without fighting back.

She was supposed to be tough and self-sufficient and in the driver's seat. The pilot's seat, actually. The former Air Force Captain was an action woman. Giving in had been the beginning of her end. The lid slammed shut, her world dimmed and then went black and she'd become acutely aware of the staleness of the air and the all-encompassing heat. Then a beam of light appeared, shining directly toward her face. She gazed up to see a video camera had been rigged to record her suffering. *Fuck this to hell.*

If she died choking on her own vomit, she wouldn't suffer enough, Stephanos had said as he'd tightened the storage tank lid. Every word uttered from his twisted lips delivered a cruel bite. She'd asked him why he was holding her captive, never expecting to receive such a chilling response.

Killing her in a slow and torturous manner was his prime objective, he had said. There would be no negotiations, no funds delivered in exchange for her safety. These men didn't want money or attention, they wanted to victimize her as an example to the Navy SEALs who had disrupted their plans.

While she was being gun-butted down to the beach, the two bastards had boasted about their affiliation with the Muslim Alliance and said they had been the instigators of numerous brutal murders witnessed by unsuspecting TV watchers. Every sinew in her body down to her bones screamed with terror once she realized who held her captive. She'd seen first hand what these monsters were capable of. Would they saw off her head, slice off her fingers one by one or leave her somewhere to die of exposure? Either way, she had known a prolonged, agonizing death was in store for her.

The men had laughed and exchanged jokes while heaving the container down to the beach and loading her onto the *Ionian Gypsy*. Below deck in the suffocating heat, she'd squirmed and struggled to free her hands and feet from her bonds.

It had been bad enough listening to the swimmers' happy banter, but it had been sheer agony hearing them splashing around the boat. Her mouth was dry as sandpaper, her tongue parched. She would have given up anything for a dip in the cool Ionian Sea to quench the heat that minute by minute, stole a little more life from her limbs.

Onboard the boat, she'd felt a flicker of hope. Maybe the phony guides' surly demeanor would alarm the swimmers. Maybe someone would search the boat and find her. But the swimmers seemed so content in each other's company they barely reacted to the rudeness.

The swimmers had embarked on a long swim from Kalamos to Kastos Island. Shortly after they'd jumped overboard and begun their channel crossing, the so-called escort boat had abandoned the group and headed toward land. Once on Kastos Island, the terrorists had unloaded her from the boat like a worthless piece of garbage. They'd dropped her into the sand, sending a jarring jolt through every bone in her body and then they had laughed and walked away, leaving her inside the scorching plastic walls to rot in the afternoon sun.

After the swimmers had stroked their way to the beach, they'd spoken in their chirpy, British accents, congratulating each other on completing the five-kilometer swim.

They'd raved about how deep blue the water looked as they crossed the channel and the lovely fish and interesting limestone formations they'd seen while following the coastline. They were experiencing beauty while she was absorbed in her hellish world of slowly dying.

Harsh commands from Stephanos had sent the group of swimmers clambering back aboard the boat. After the engine had roared to life, its sound had slowly faded until all she heard was the splash of the sea.

The absence of the swimmers' happy banter seemed to mock her. Hearing them talk about the dolphins they'd seen and how refreshing the water felt on the hot day hadn't nearly approached the torture of realizing all hope of being rescued had been lost.

The slosh of the sea waves on the sand had never made her feel so alone. And helpless. She could almost hear a ticking clock in her head reminding her that time was running out, that death was about to take her into it's irreversible embrace.

Damn it. She wasn't accustomed to depending on others. *If only I could get out of here, I'd chase down those bastards and beat the shit out of them.*

Now all she could do was thrash around until her ankles and wrists bled from the ropes binding and cutting into her skin. Even if she found a way to shuck the bonds, it was unlikely she'd be able to escape the confining walls of the tank.

I'm out of options. If the suffocating heat didn't finish her off, dehydration would. She slid her tongue over her parched lips. Every swallow incited a cough. Her throat felt like leather that had been dried in the sun. Stiff, rigid, with not even a drop of saliva to lubricate it.

She glanced up at the video camera, wishing her hands were free so she could smash it to smithereens. For a while she'd forgotten about it, she'd been so caught up in her circumstances. But all at once, its presence enraged her. While she lay there suffocating and coming closer and closer to death, every agonized facial expression, every second of her demise was being recorded.

Fuck this. The documentation of her suffering would be a huge victory for the terrorists. *If you hide your suffering until the end, no one will want to watch this goddamned clip.* Baylee ground her teeth together, determined not to groan or grimace. She tried to think about something calming. Something that would distract her mind from the gut-wrenching lump inside her stomach, the fire that burned in her lungs, the throbbing headache that made her forehead feel like it would burst apart. *Nathan.* She closed her eyes, drew in a ravaged breath and imagined being wrapped tightly in his arms. *Safe, warm, comforted. That's what I want to think about until this ends.*

CHAPTER TWELVE

May 25, 2016
Lefkada Island, Greece
1545 hours

Jamie jogged down the steep path toward the beach with Karl and the two swimmers. The team of police officers, military and FBI agents were busy searching the *Ionian Gypsy*. Officer Laskaris looked up and shouted, "I need you to stay back."

Karl took a step ahead of the others. "It's urgent that we speak with you. These two women, Christine and Lisa, were on board that boat today. They observed suspicious activities. I take it Baylee's not on board?"

Officer Laskaris shook his head. "We searched every inch of the boat and didn't find a scrap of evidence that indicates any hostage has been on board." He walked toward the narrowest part of the bow and jumped onto the dock, striding toward Karl and the others. He plucked a notebook from his lapel pocket and snapped it open. "I'm ready to listen to whatever you've got to tell me."

The two women shared everything they had previously shared with Jamie and Karl.

Officer Laskaris removed his sunglasses and wiped away sweat with the back of his hand before sliding them back over the bridge of his nose. "That seems very suspicious. If Ms. Stiles has been abandoned inside that water storage tank, she won't last long in this heat. We need to get to Kastos Island right away. Do you have any idea where your regular guides went?"

Both of the women spoke at once in loud, anxious voices. They stopped to look at each other and Christine waved her hand for Lisa to go ahead.

"No. We were told a maintenance issue had come up with the boat, but Kallistos and Alexios seemed edgy and preoccupied and quickly disembarked once we returned to the dock. They had to have been dealing with more than a simple boat repair."

Jamie paced across the sand, sharing her impressions of the situation. "What if the two phony guides contacted Kallistos and gave him some urgent reason to return. Once he returned to the dock, maybe these men were waiting and kidnapped or even murdered him." Jamie paused and raised her hand in the air. "Or maybe Kallistos and Alexios were accomplices to the kidnapping."

Officer Laskaris nodded. "You could be right. I'll tell the others what we've uncovered here. We'll assemble a party to contact the families and query hotel employees to dig up leads on Kallistos and Alexios's whereabouts while the rest of us head to Kastos Island." He directed his gaze toward Christine and Lisa. "Can you ladies describe the beach where you completed your swim?"

The two women nodded in unison and Christine spoke first. "It was on a beach on the far side of the island."

"Are you absolutely certain of that?"

"Yes, we could see the Greek mainland from where we finished our swim." Lisa pulled her water camera, secured by a lanyard around her neck, over her head and pushed a button. Then she extended her arm, holding the camera toward him and pointing at a photo. "Here's a shot of the beach on Kastos Island where we finished."

He took the camera from her hand and squinted at the screen. "Those pictures are tiny. I can't see much of anything in this light."

"The part of the island where we swam seemed mostly deserted," said Christine. "We passed a hut or two here and there as we swam along the coast and saw a few small brown mountain goats walking the hillsides a bit before we landed. I'm quite sure I could point out the area from a boat."

Officer Laskaris crossed his arms over his chest and adopted an erect, confrontational stance. "We're dealing with a terrorist organization here. It would be much too dangerous to take you two out on that boat. I'm going to have to ask you to turn that camera over to me, Miss. We're going to need to download those images."

"Yeah, ok—" Lisa frowned when he took the camera from her hand.

"That will just waste more time. Why can't they go along?" Jamie asked in an irritated tone of voice. "You wouldn't have a thing to go on without Christine and Lisa's help. There are enough armed men around to protect them. And you need them. Not only do they seem to know where Baylee is being held, they can also identify the kidnappers."

"I see your point, Miss Phillips. But there's no telling what we could run into during our approach. Another boat might pursue us or a sniper might be hunkered down on that island just waiting for us." He paused and uncrossed his arms, letting his hands fall to his sides. "As long as you keep your heads down during our approach, it should be all right. But I'll have to run it by the others. This is a team effort."

"I understand." Jamie pressed her lips tightly together, trying to reign in her excitement.

"We'd be glad to make the journey if you think it would help," said Christine.

"It might. Let me go clear this with the others." Officer Laskaris stuffed the notebook back in his lapel pocket and pinned Jamie and Karl with a stare. "But there's no reason for you two to tag along."

Jamie's shoulders sagged with disappointment and she spoke in a resigned voice. "I guess you're right." There wasn't a single logical reason she and Karl should go along, but the thought of missing out on all the action frustrated her. They were hot on a solid lead and she would have liked to know the minute Baylee had been found.

Nathan hopped off the boat and strode toward them. His head lowered, his nostrils flaring with anger, he looked like a charging bull.

Karl walked toward him and placed a hand on his shoulder. "Hang in there, big guy. These ladies were aboard the *Ionian Gypsy* this afternoon. They think they know where the MA are holding Baylee."

Nathan's dark brows drew together and he scowled. He clearly had no patience for small talk or introductions. "Then why the hell aren't we moving?"

*

Nathan could barely contain the fury simmering inside of him. He'd always prided himself on his easy-going demeanor and controlled temper. But today, he was a man changed by circumstance. Someone had stolen his woman and that wasn't okay.

Rescuing Baylee before anyone harmed her mattered more than food, water or the next breath. A close second was tracking down the men who had kidnapped her and ripping every fiber of flesh from their miserable bones. *The bastards.*

"What's the hold up?" he asked impatiently. He'd walked to the bow and waited for the go ahead to unhitch the boat from its mooring. It had taken long enough for the police officer to convince the Deltas and the FBI agents to take the two swimmers along for the search. Why wouldn't it be okay? They seemed to be the only ones that had a clue what was happening.

The FBI agents and the Deltas acted like they were the shit, but they hadn't even thought to question the swimmers. They'd queried the boat driver, but after finding no evidence Baylee had been on board, they'd let him walk away instead of detaining him for further questioning.

He wished Karl had been allowed on board. If he and Jamie hadn't stopped the swimmers and questioned them, they'd be nowhere with this. At least Darryl was here. His best friend would be the only calming force as this terrifying ordeal played out.

"We'll be on our way in a flash," said Officer Karaholios. Mike's starting up the engines as fast as he can."

As fast as he can doesn't do it for me. Nathan squatted down and cracked his knuckles before gripping the ropes. Seconds seemed like hours. *Hurry the fuck up. I wish he'd let me fire up this goddamn miserable excuse for a boat. It probably won't have a damn bit of pickup.*

He knew their reason for taking the tour boat. If they jetted off in the sleek and speedy watercraft the Deltas had arrived in, it would draw too much attention. Special Operations groups didn't often operate in broad daylight, but by some miracle his former Chief had gone to bat for him and organized this unconventional mission.

He could have been stuck searching for Baylee with just the Greek police to support him. He couldn't imagine much crime ever happened in this boon dock village. They'd probably forgotten how to fire their weapons and spent most days drinking coffee or taking siestas. He knew he should be counting himself lucky he had Delta and FBI support, but impatience was driving him close to the edge.

After the engine roared to life, Nathan unhitched the mooring from the dock and dropped the ropes on the bow before plopping down on one of the four enormous blue beanbag chairs on the bow deck.

Darryl dropped down onto the chair beside him and slung an arm around Nathan's shoulder. "I know waiting is frustrating as hell. I remember how it felt when I found out Olivia had been kidnapped in Italy. We're on our way, Nathan. Get your head together so once we hit land, you're one hundred percent focused. You got it?"

"Got it," said Nathan without conviction. If anyone understood his predicament right now, it was Darryl. When the life of the woman he loved had been at stake, he'd been anything but focused. Chief Drake had nearly shit his pants when Darryl had spilled out his feelings about Olivia in the middle of the most critical part of the extraction operation. But in the end, he'd pulled his shit together and prevailed.

I've got to shut down my fucking feelings and pretend this is another routine hostage rescue. He'd been the tough man so many times. *I can handle this.* Once their jeep had broken down in a remote part of the Iraqi desert and six of them, including Darryl, had walked over dunes and dirt for days without food or water. There hadn't been complaining or even an undercurrent of *we can't do this*, it was put one dusty boot in front of the other until they reached a village or died.

Since enlisting in the Navy, Nathan had been shot, stabbed and beaten senseless on various missions, yet not once had he felt as panicked as he did now. On missions, it was all about getting a job done. Emotions played no role in his actions.

Now his emotions threatened to paralyze him. He was too involved in what was happening to keep his mind centered. He'd seen firsthand what emotional involvement had done to Darryl. Being too involved with the rescue victim had impaired his judgment and nearly led to a perilous outcome.

Nathan's mind was lost in thought as the *Ionian Gypsy* skipped across the water and bounced over the deep blue waves. He barely noticed the thickly vegetated islands shifting position or the water breaking over the bow and splashing his face as the seas grew rougher. His eyes unfocused, he saw Baylee's face clearly in his mind.

He had memorized the configuration of every single freckle that dotted the fair skin on her face, the way her pale blond hair changed color depending on the time of the day. Under the sunlight, the ends of her hair looked like white fire. So intense. Like her personality. She was all energy and spontaneity with the tendency to change moods with the wind. He pictured her laughing, her head thrown back, her hair scattered in every direction. That's how he wanted to see her now. He didn't want to picture her begging for her life while a madman held a gun to her head or a sharp blade to her jugular.

He now understood how Baylee had felt that night she'd snuck out of their Paris hotel room and planned to leave him. The fiancé she'd loved before she'd met Nathan had died suddenly during a running race and she'd endured an aftermath of suffering.

Three years later, she'd met a Navy SEAL who faced death every time he went wheels up. She'd been haunted by thoughts that once again, she might end up alone and empty and missing the man that she loved.

Nathan had tracked her down; desperate to know the truth about why she'd left. After finding her alone and crying in the airport, he had voiced his deep feelings for her. He had known all along it was a risky move and that more than likely he'd end up walking away alone. Not many women could cope with the trials of a relationship with a SEAL. But in the end, Baylee had chosen to stick it out. She loved him and didn't want to face a life without him even if they had to spend long periods of time apart and their time together might be cut short if he were killed.

Now the situation had been reversed and Nathan faced the possibility of the unthinkable—that he might never see Baylee alive again.

He wanted to hear her eardrum piercing voice as she sassed off someone who had treated her like she weren't capable. He wanted to sift his fingers through wisps of her platinum blonde hair.

He couldn't stand the thought that he might never again see her plant her hands on her hips and give him that quirky smile that showed her displeasure with whatever he'd just said—just before she gave him an earful about it. And that he might never again hold that bundle of feminine fury in his arms and make love to her.

"Over there, that's where we landed."

Christine's comment broke into his thoughts and he glanced up, his eyes gaining focus and taking in the island in front of him, where white limestone cliffs steeply dipped into the sea on either side of a small beach.

The place looked nearly deserted. He'd seen nothing but a ramshackle house here and there to indicate the island was inhabited. More goats seemed to reside on the island than people. This seemed to be the beach no one frequented, the place the terrorists had apparently determined was the ideal location to leave someone to die a slow and painful death. His fists clenched, he ground his teeth together not caring whether it cramped his jaw or pulverized his molars. *Baylee's on this island. And I have to get to her.*

CHAPTER THIRTEEN

May 25, 2016
Lefkada Island, Greece
1605 hours

Strands of Jamie's breeze blown hair tickled Karl's cheek as he stood on the beach beside her, watching the *Ionian Gypsy* slice through the too-blue water and scatter a wake of cerulean blue water behind it. His ears perceived the Doppler effect in action as the roar of the motor deepened to a lower frequency and faded out until he heard only the chatter of curious onlookers and the watery sound of small waves striking the sand.

The late afternoon sunlight transformed the tips of Jamie's unruly hair a fiery gold. He was eager to resume their conversation, but wanted her to say something first. If he burst out with a declaration of love, he'd risk having his heart broken all over again.

Karl thrived on order and detailed planning. He'd booked his plane ticket and room reservations in Athens and Lefkada, expecting to spend any time he wasn't hanging out with his friends playing war games on his computer.

With his mind fully engaged on tactical strategies, the blinds drawn, he wouldn't be tempted to think about what his ex-girlfriend was or wasn't wearing on the beach or in a nearby room.

Fate had sabotaged Karl's orderly plan. He'd run into Jamie almost immediately after arrival in Lefkada, Baylee had been kidnapped, and images of him and Jamie naked and sweaty under the sheets continued to flash through his mind.

For months, he'd shoved his feelings into the deepest recesses of his brain. He'd never been comfortable with emotions. Logic and reason were so much safer to live with than deep and unpredictable feelings.

The instant he'd seen Jamie standing in the hotel lobby, all the emotions he'd worked so hard to bury, that he'd developed a methodology for keeping under cover, had burst out in a painful emotional array of colors.

Now that they had resurfaced, there seemed to be no stuffing them back down, despite the arsenal of logic and reasoning he'd tried to apply.

He'd called her out in front of the others without thinking. It had been an emotionally driven outburst, a release of frustration over losing her. It had been so out-of-character and mean spirited, but for some reason he hadn't been able to stop it. Runaway emotions seemed to have gotten the best of him.

Maybe all this chaos would end if he could get some closure, if he could find out once and for all what had been behind their sudden break up.

Does she still love me was the question he wanted answered. Even his logical mind had processed signs that suggested she might still have feelings for him. *If only she'd say something.*

As the minutes ticked by in silence, he considered telling her his plans to resign from the Navy. *It's too risky.* He'd been on the brink of telling her when she'd called off their relationship. A knife slicing into his skin would have hurt less. A bloody wound, unless lethal, would eventually heal but his wounded heart hurt every bit as badly as the first day she'd struck him with those final words.

He pressed his lips together, vowing not to say something that might worsen his suffering.

"Hey, Karl, I know you're worried about Baylee, but you look more upset than ever. Is there something else bothering you?" Jamie looked at him with that compassionate wide-eyed expression. Those intelligent blue eyes of hers had always seemed to see into him, to see what no one else bothered to notice. When they'd been together, he'd cherished her insight. Now it felt threatening. Containing his feelings felt like the only way to maintain his sanity. And his pride. He glanced at the ground, donning a serious expression. *Does she know I'm still in love with her?*

How could he hold it against her that she'd broken it off? Dating a SEAL was no picnic. He'd been deployed for months at a time and had returned stateside exhausted and often out-of-sorts.

Despite the long separations and the disintegration of the closeness they'd once shared, it seemed neither of them really wanted to let go. He'd criticized Jamie for her display of jealousy, but he would have been equally upset if he'd seen her on the arm of a strange man. Why had he said that she should let him find someone else? The only woman he wanted was Jamie.

He'd recently sworn that he'd remain the perpetual bachelor. The lone SEAL member to stay with the Navy until his hair grayed and he walked with a limp. Until Drake or his successor had to pat him on the back and say it was time to hang up the uniform. Now he could only think about how much he wanted Jamie back in his life.

"Karl, I asked you what's wrong. Why won't you answer me?"

He looked up to meet her inquisitive gaze. He hadn't meant to wait so long to respond, but he'd gotten lost in thought. "It's just been a rough day that's all." Karl studied Jamie's profile as she swung her gaze toward the *Ionian Gypsy* that now looked the size of a toy boat far away on the vast sea of water. She looked more beautiful than ever with her wind-messed hair and her pale, freckled cheeks flushed by the sun.

She frowned and twirled a strand of hair around one finger. "That's for sure. I wish I'd stayed home."

"Oh?" Her statement caught him by surprise and bruised his ego at the same time.

Jamie tilted her head slightly to the side and as she spoke, her lips quivered. "I never imagined seeing you again would hurt this bad. And then in the lobby, when I saw you—" Tears filled her eyes.

He wasn't sure how to interpret her sudden burst of emotions. Was she confessing she still loved him or expressing her disdain over having to deal with this uncomfortable encounter with their past? "Why did it hurt, Jamie? I don't understand."

"Because I still love you, that's why."

He felt as if all the air had been pulled from his chest. "You still love me?" he whispered. A minute earlier, he'd imagined pulling her tightly into his arms and confessing what he'd planned for their future if he'd heard those words. The words clung to his tongue, unwilling to leave his mouth. Instead of reaching for her, he stood frozen like a Greek statue, not moving, not speaking.

She has a funny way of showing she loves me, telling me she wants to date other people. Once again, he was an unwitting passenger on this roller coaster ride of changing emotions he couldn't seem to control.

Every fiber in his body wanted Jamie back in his life again, but the trust had been compromised. He needed to feel some sense of security before he allowed physical attraction and desire to take over.

Jamie wiped a tear from the corner of her eyes. "Is it too late?"

Karl took a step closer, gazing at the ground, intending to say or do something, he wasn't sure what. Maybe he'd place his hands gently on her arms and gently say *no, it's not too late.* Or he would resist touching her, but gaze deeply into her eyes and say in a few words that he wanted to try again without getting too emotional.

He dropped his hands to his sides when a group of men appeared on the hill above them. *Talk about bad timing.* Sighing, he stepped off to the side to let them pass. He wondered if they'd found the two missing guides.

Their conversation could wait long enough for him to ask what was happening with Baylee. Karl cleared his throat and turned toward the man leading the group. He guessed from his bulging muscles and buzz cut, he was Delta Force. "Have they found her?"

"No, not yet. I just received word that the boat's approaching Kastos Island now."

Karl turned toward Jamie, feeling guilty that he hadn't responded to her candid emotional display. "I—" He frowned when he saw only footprints where she'd stood beside him seconds ago. Already several feet away, she was making a stormy retreat up the beach toward the hotel. They'd been within an arm's reach of an understanding. Now it all seemed lost. Karl swung his arm through the air and swore.

"Did we interrupt something?" The soldier's lips twisted into a knowing smile.

"Yeah, kind of, but don't worry about it," Karl said through clenched teeth.

The man motioned for the others to continue back down to the beach. "I'll catch up with you in a minute." He turned toward Karl. "I'm Jake Dunbar by the way."

"Karl Patterson. I'd appreciate it if you shared what you know. Once my friend calms down, I'm sure she'll want to know more about what's going on with Baylee."

"She's pretty pissed off for a friend," said Jake.

"Yeah, well I don't want to talk about it."

"We found Kallistos and Alexios bound and gagged in an empty room. Other than a few bruises and scratches, they're unharmed. Apparently someone made a cell phone call to Kallistos reporting his wife and daughter had been seriously injured in a car accident. He and Alexios were running up the trail from the beach when they were ambushed."

"Were their captors familiar to either of them?"

"If they're telling the truth, no. They reported that the two terrorists spoke in Arabic and seemed to be of Middle Eastern descent. I really can't say more than that."

"I'm on a special operations team. I know these terrorists are MA and that they are targeting Nathan and our SEAL Team. If it weren't for us, they wouldn't bother to cause trouble on this island."

"They tracked you here? That's some shit," said Jake.

"Yeah, a pile of it. And to think that I almost turned down the invitation to this wedding."

Jake laughed. "You're here for a wedding? Who's the lucky guy?"

"Darryl Jennings. You must have met him earlier."

"Yeah, I did. Getting embroiled in an extraction mission is one hell of a way to kick off the wedding. He should be drunk as a skunk and hiring naked women to do a dance routine for him."

"I don't think so. Baylee's his best friend's girlfriend. He'll be with Nathan until this ends."

The man shifted uneasily on his feet, clearly uncomfortable continuing with the idle chatter. "I need to get down there."

"What will you do now? Wait around until they get back?"

"Hell no. We'll hire an inconspicuous looking boat to Kastos Island and get in on the action. I could probably persuade the guys to let you come along."

Karl looked longingly toward the ocean. The instinct to jump into the action burned in his blood. He could already imagine leaping on the boat deck and adrenaline surging through his veins. *What about Jamie?* His head swung toward the path where her footprints had carved angry impressions in the sand.

Karl's commitment to his SEAL Team brother was strong. If his participation would increase the chances of Baylee being returned safe, he would jump on Jake's offer, but he knew they'd arrive after-the-fact anyway. He wouldn't be shirking any duty staying behind and resolving the conflict with Jamie.

"Thanks for the offer, but I'll pass. There are plenty of good men on the job and as you noticed, I've got another situation clamoring for my attention." He directed his gaze up the path. Jamie had already disappeared behind the tree-covered ridge.

"She looks like a handful. Good luck," said Jake.

Karl strode up the beach and followed the winding path up the steep hill that led to the hotel, debating about how he would approach his angry ex-girlfriend. After batting a pine branch out of the way, he jerked his head up when he saw motion out of the corner of his eye.

"Oh, sorry, I didn't see you." Karl noticed Olivia had jumped off the path to keep from being mowed down.

"Don't worry. I'm good at quick evasions," said Olivia. Her smile melted away and creases appeared on her smooth white forehead. "Is something going on? I saw three police cars parked in front of the hotel and a black SUV with tinted windows that looked suspiciously like a secret-service vehicle."

There would be no watering down his report for the no-nonsense CIA agent. "Baylee's been kidnapped. Local Delta Force and FBI have been called in to collaborate with the local police."

"Where are Nathan and Darryl?"

"On a boat headed for Kastos Island where they believe she's being held."

"Damn, that's awful." Olivia's lips drew into a thin line and she paused before speaking again. "Why would someone kidnap Baylee?"

"These men are with the Muslim Alliance."

"That's even worse news. They're a ruthless bunch of bastards. I never would have imagined they'd have a presence on such a quiet island like this."

"They're here for a reason, Olivia. They know everything about us. We've targeted them on many recent missions. Someone must have followed us at some point and gleaned information about our whereabouts and activities. Their sole purpose is revenge, which they clearly outlined in a note delivered to Nathan. They want to use Baylee as an example to avenge the damage we've inflicted on their organization."

"Do you know where she's being held?"

He shared the important details of his encounter with the recreational swimmers.

"Is Kastos Island close by?"

"No, it's more than an hour's boat ride. You can't see it from this beach. It's obscured by Skorpios Island. Out there." He pointed toward the island, which had once been owned by Aristotle and Jackie Onassis and was later sold to a Russian billionaire and gifted to his daughter.

Olivia glanced toward the ocean and her dark brows drew together. The normally soft lines of her face looked so hard and determined, Karl thought she might try to swim to the island if she weren't presented with better options.

"It would be safer to stay here. But if you're hell bent on going out there, one of the Delta Force guys is going to hire a b—" Karl allowed his arm to collapse at his side. There was no point in finishing his sentence. Olivia was already sprinting down the path toward the beach.

CHAPTER FOURTEEN

May 25, 2016
Lefkada Island, Greece
1615 hours

Jamie shoved an all-terrain sandal-clad foot under the outdoor shower tilting it different angles to rinse off the sand. Not caring much whether she'd done a thorough job, she jerked that foot out and stuck the other one under the rain of water. After hastily rinsing the second foot, she cranked off the water and strode along the stone walkway toward her building.

"I never should have come here," she said under her breath as she stomped up the stairs to her room. She wanted to lock herself inside and not come out until the wedding was over and everyone had checked out. That way she wouldn't have to see Karl again, she wouldn't have to face her feelings and she wouldn't have to suffer the humiliation of having everyone see that after all this time, she still hadn't gotten over their break up.

Karl said he wanted to listen. And maybe he did...If there wasn't anything more pressing to deal with at the time. Everything seemed to take priority over their relationship. Even off duty, he was distracted. She sighed, feeling frustrated.

Why am I acting so selfish? Of course he's distracted. The guys on the Team are like family to him. Nathan's going through hell now — it makes sense that Karl would want to be there for him. That's what drew me to him in the first place, the fact that he cared about people.

His willingness to help others was one of his finest qualities. During the Paris fire, he had rescued a young boy and another woman before rushing back into the building for Jamie. Rescuing her from the fire hadn't been part of his job description, but if he'd paused to talk to bystanders instead of returning to the building for her, she wouldn't be alive now.

I should cut him some slack. Damn it. Instead of storming off, she should have stuck around for an update on Baylee. She didn't usually act crazy in relationships even though she'd dated her share of men. None of the others had mattered much, but for some reason Karl had stuck to her heart like glue.

She pulled open the door to her room and stepped inside. After slamming the door shut, she strode toward the bed and threw herself down onto the hard mattress, buried her face in a pillow and sobbed. Tears flowed like rivers and she clutched the covers tightly with her fists.

She didn't try to suppress her sobs, to slow the rush of tears that dampened the pillow. Releasing her pain numbed her brain. It took the edge off of thoughts about the breakup, the pain of seeing Karl again, the misdirected jealousy and the frustration over not knowing whether he still wanted her. The loud, wet crying marathon soothed her, gradually bringing her back to a state of equilibrium.

I feel so much better now. Her mind relaxed, she felt calm enough to objectively evaluate what had gone wrong with her and Karl.

She released her death grip on the covers and wrapped her arms around the pillow, hugging it close. Karl was probably on a boat to Kastos Island by now. *Unless he decided to come after me.* The thought thrilled and frightened her at the same time. She wanted him to care enough to chase after her, but she didn't want him to see her swollen face, to know how much this situation had upset her.

She planted her chin on the pillow and gazed at the headboard. The long separations had dealt a significant blow, causing them to drift apart. Their mutual lack of experience with serious relationships had led to secondary problems.

She felt sure he, too, had fallen victim to roller coaster emotions. That wasn't a comfortable place to be for people accustomed to being in control. Both of them were reacting too much without thinking about the consequences of those sudden bursts of emotions. And the result had been pain, misunderstanding and the end of their relationship.

Intuition snapped her back to their last phone conversation. The more she thought about it, the more she believed Karl had planned to share something of importance when she'd blurted out her dating other people suggestion. When their relationship had taken a turn for the worse, it had been a major confidence breaker. She'd assumed he'd wanted her out of his life.

He'd spoken more rapidly than she'd ever heard him speak before. Had he been keyed up and nervous about what he wanted to say? *If only I'd let him speak first, damn it.*

What had he planned to say? That was the question she wanted answered more than anything. Maybe he'd been about to suggest how they could improve their relationship. Maybe he hadn't found it to be a nuisance and she hadn't done him any favor at all by calling it off.

I should have asked what he wanted before saying what I did. If her hunch were right, no wonder he had acted so silent and distant after she'd suggested they call it quits. He'd been ready with a plan to fix things and she'd shot holes in it before he had a chance to speak.

Damn. I have to do something. She knew it wouldn't be easy. She had no experience with patching up things with men. Any other break up she'd had in the past had come too late and hadn't been something she'd want to reverse. She'd apologize and if confronted with a harsh response, she'd control her impulses and try not to overreact.

She jerked her head up from the pillow at the sound of a knock. *Please let it be him.* "Who is it?"

"It's Karl. I know you're upset, but I had to know if there was any new information on Baylee. Please. I'm ready to listen. There'll be no more distractions."

His sincerity moved her. Most men wouldn't risk speaking their mind like that in a hotel hallway where he was likely to be overhead. But Karl had no need to worry that expressing a few words would compromise his masculinity. Sensitive side or not, he was one hundred percent man. He didn't give a damn what anyone thought. He acted according to his values and to Jamie that was sexy as hell.

Tremors of excitement raced through her veins. Jamie peeled her face off the damp pillow and pushed herself up off the bed. She walked to the door and swung it open to see Karl standing there. She read so many emotions on that face she loved so much—frustration, confusion, sadness. Even his eyes changed shades of blue as his emotions shifted. She hung her head, embarrassed by her swollen, red eyes. "Come in. I'm sorry. I shouldn't have stormed off like that. It's just—" She wasn't sure how to finish. *She wanted to say I don't know why I'm acting like such a freak lately.*

He strode into the room and brushed a hand over the back of a chair.

"Why don't you sit for a minute?" Jamie asked. "I think we both need to try to have a normal conversation."

An awkward laugh escaped his lips. "Yeah, okay." He pulled back a chair and dropped into it, glancing at the floor and then pressing his lips tightly together. "I'm not sure I can deliver on this normal conversation suggestion. You're not just an ordinary person to me."

Jamie sighed and walked toward him, pulling up a chair and sitting in front of him so their knees nearly touched. "Karl, I'm sorry. I haven't handled our relationship at all well. I've been acting crazy. Like a love sick teenager. I'd like to blame it on my lack of experience. The other relationships I've had in the past just didn't matter to me like this."

"If this relationship matters to you, Jamie... Why did you end it?"

The pain she saw in his eyes made her chest ache. "I don't know," she said in a desperate voice. "Like I said earlier, I made a mistake." She reached for Karl's hand taking comfort in its strength and warmth. She traced a finger over a knuckle and the large muscular expanse of his hand. A tremor of attraction jolted through her body. She missed the intimacy they had once shared. She recalled how his hands had held her tight until morning, how they had explored her body and sent wanton heat scattering everywhere. She ached to feel Karl's touch. "I never stopped loving you, Karl. I only said what I did because I thought it was what you wanted."

Karl's eyes widened and he shook his head. "How could you imagine that?"

"I don't know. You always seemed so exhausted and distracted whenever we got together. I felt like our relationship had become like a chore to you."

Karl's voice rang with distress and regret. "Oh, no, Jamie. I had no idea you felt that way. That was never how I felt. I wish you would have said something."

Fate seemed to always get in the way. It had prevented them from meeting when they were students at Clemson University. Oh, she'd seen him on campus in passing and he'd seen her she later learned, but neither of them had taken the gutsy initiative to walk up to the other and start a conversation. Even after they'd found each other in Paris of all places, fate had pulled them apart with misunderstanding.

To hell with fate. I'm going to take control of my life. "Looking back, I know I did the wrong thing not sharing my concerns about the relationship and asking what you thought we should do about it.

"But we spent so much time apart and after a while I didn't feel as comfortable talking to you as before. I know it sounds strange, but even when we were together, it started to feel like we weren't really together because our minds were too far apart.

"I almost said something a few times but felt awkward bringing it up. The last time we talked, well, I decided if I really loved you, I should let you go instead of hanging on when I wasn't what you wanted anymore."

Karl reached for her hands and gripped them tight, massaging her wrists with his thumbs. "Jamie, no. My feelings for you never changed."

Never changed? Her heart raced and the thrill of what he had just said stole her ability to think clearly.

"Did you hear what I said?"

Jamie nodded. "Yes, Karl, I'm so sorry. About everything. All those months apart were so miserable."

"I missed you, too, Jamie. It was tough to focus on my work when you were constantly on my mind."

"You thought about me?"

He planted a gentle kiss on her forehead. "Of course I did. Every single day."

Jamie told him how she had wished so badly he would call she sometimes dreamed he'd called and had more than once imagined hearing a ringing phone when it was only the backbeat of a song in a nearby office or the whine of a passing vehicle.

"I would have done anything to keep you from hurting like this. From now on let's not let misunderstandings get in the way of what we have."

"I promise I'll do better from now on."

"Sit with me." Karl reached for her and when she moved closer, he wrapped his arms around her waist and pulled her into his lap.

Leaning against his sturdy chest and secured by his strong arms, she felt safe. "But there's something I have to ask you."

"Sure anything." His hot breath tickled her neck.

"Whenever I recall our last conversation and believe me, I've rehearsed it in my head a thousand times, the more I've been sure there was something important you wanted to say to me. Am I right?" She craned her neck so she could see his face.

A wry grin raised one corner of his mouth. "Yes, Jamie, you're right about that." He spoke in the gentle compassionate voice that she adored. "But what I planned to say to you was serious. I'm not sure you're ready for that."

Serious? Had he planned to make a commitment to me? She couldn't stand not knowing a second longer. "Tell me, Karl. Tell me what you were going to—"

The thunder of machine gun fire in the hallway outside cut her off. She instinctively jumped and Karl reacted in an instant, gripping her by the shoulders, pulling her down onto the floor and shielding her with his body. "Stay down."

As the staccato of gunfire continued, a bullet burst through the center of the room door, scattering wood fragments across the door. Another hit a wall, knocking a photo of Santorini Island onto the floor.

Jamie trembled with terror. "Oh, my God, what the hell is happening?"

"Don't worry, I've got you covered." Karl pulled her in closer, smoothing his hands over her trembling body.

She reached for Karl's hand and tugged on it. "Let's crawl under the bed. It'll be safer over there."

Karl continued to shield her as more rounds of gunfire were exchanged and they squirmed their way across the floor. "Go ahead," Karl urged as he waited for her to push herself into the narrow space underneath the bed before wedging himself in behind her.

By now the gunfire and shouts had ceased and there was only silence and the sound of their heavy breathing in the confined space.

Karl reached for her, tracing a finger over her face.

"This hasn't been the best day for talking," said Jamie. "Everything's crazy around here. I wonder what's going on now."

"If you promise to stay here, I'll go check it out."

"No, Karl, that wouldn't be safe."

"I've got a pistol, don't worry."

"Yes, but those men had automatic weapons."

"I have to make sure my friends aren't out there injured or dead."

Jamie knew Karl could handle himself in a dangerous situation and was willing to compromise. "Fine, I'll stay, but please be careful. Our conversation isn't over."

Karl kissed her gently on the lips before sliding out from underneath the bed. "No, it isn't. I'll be back as soon as I can."

CHAPTER FIFTEEN

May 25, 2016
Kastos Island, Greece
1645 hours

Thoughts of Nathan were Baylee's only comfort, her only distraction from the all-encompassing pain. In her mind, she lay beside him in on a pillow top mattress in Prague, on a grassy lawn in Paris, anywhere except in this scorching hot water tank. She closed her eyes and imagined him tracing a finger over her cheek and saying *I love you* before she drifted into sleep.

As her head swirled in delirium, the pain she'd previously felt seemed to dissipate into an intoxicating haze. Her fantasies about her and

Nathan appeared in brighter colors with sharper edges until she was almost convinced they were real.

In her fantasy, they'd discarded their swimsuits and were exploring each other's bodies while they stood in chest deep water, allowing the refreshing Ionian Sea to splash over them. She wiggled her foot around in the sand beneath her feet, catching a rounded pebble between her toes. *The water's so cool. So cool.*

Over there, Nathan seemed to say. *What is he talking about?*

She thought she heard other men's voices. *Darryl? What is he doing here? I should put my swimsuit back on. This could be awkward.* She reminded herself none of this was real. Her brain had to be releasing sedating brain chemicals, making her hallucinate about rescuers so death wouldn't feel so frightening.

Tears that would have flowed because of the pain of everything she was losing had run dry. "Goodbye, Nathan," she rasped. Her parched throat burned like fire uttering those simple words. Yet it wasn't enough. She had to voice to herself what was in her heart one last time. "I love you."

"Did you hear that, Darryl?"

There's his voice again. Nathan's resonant voice pitched upward the way it always did when he was excited. *I'm imagining things. That can't really be Nathan's voice.* But if intoxicating brain chemicals were responsible for what she had heard, they weren't lessening the pain of losing him. Her chest felt like an empty hollow thinking she'd never see him again. No. Baylee curled tighter into a ball, seeking the comfort of her own touch, as she imagined Nathan's hand stroking her thighs instead of her own. Strong, protecting, sensual.

Her whole world shook and vibrated and men shouted and gave orders. Dizziness overpowered her, her stomach roiled and she wretched. *I've lost my mind. Please let this torture end.*

She felt a rush of a sea breeze and looked up to see a burst of blue sky above her. It's too blue to be real, she thought. At first she thought she was dead, but then her splitting headache and the burning sensation that had spread from her mouth to her abdomen soon reminded her she was still very much alive.

Maybe the terrorists came back to finish me off. She gasped when she saw Nathan's face peering over the rim of the container opening, his steel blue eyes wide with concern. "Is it really you?" Her voice sounded strangled and alien, her throat burned too hot and dry to say anything else. She blinked again and he was still there.

"Oh, my God, Baylee. What have they done to you?" He turned away and spoke to someone. "Get me some water. Now. I'm going to lift her out."

She still wasn't sure if what she saw in front of her eyes was real or just a dream until his strong, muscular arms reached for her. He slowly raised her out of the hellish place she'd been confined, and into the paradise of his arms and the cool, moist sea breeze.

He laid her down on the sand and poured cold water on her face and into her mouth. She gasped, lapping up the cold water with delight, choking on its delicious wetness as she tried to swallow it. The sea breeze cooled her overheated skin and the scent of pine and salt tinged her nostrils. But her vision was her most keen sense at that moment. The man she loved, who she thought she'd never again see, never again touch, was there. He gazed at her with so much love, smoothing his strong hands over her skin, caring for her when she needed it most. He kissed every inch of her face and whispered, "I love you" over and over again.

CHAPTER SIXTEEN

May 25, 2016
Nikiana Hotel
Lefkada Island, Greece
1650 hours

Karl curled his finger around the trigger of his Sig Sauer as he opened the door and crept out into the hallway. He swung his head first to the right and then to the left. *No signs of movement.* After hearing several rounds of automatic weapon fire, he wasn't surprised by what he saw. Chunks of drywall strewn across the tile, bullet holes scarring the walls, bloodied bodies.

He strode toward the two bodies that littered the hallway along with fragments of what had once been the walls. He blew out a relieved sigh. Even face down, he knew for sure neither were Darryl or Nathan. He hoped they weren't friends or family here for the wedding. Curious about the identities of the victims, he flipped over the body of one man who had been shot in the head.

A stern voice reprimanded him. "Who are you? Stop, don't move."

Karl raised his hands, including the one bearing his weapon, and whirled around to see Jake, the Delta he'd spoken to earlier pointing the barrel of his weapon his way. "Jake, it's Karl. You remember me, right?"

Jake lowered his weapon and adopted a more relaxed stance. "Oh, yes, of course. My mistake. This situation has me spooked. Just when I thought it was over I heard the exchange of gunfire."

"I was in my room when all hell broke loose out here. You said it's over. Was Baylee Stiles located? Are Darryl and Nathan safe?"

Jake rubbed the back of his neck with one hand before nodding. "That's an affirmative on both accounts."

"That's a relief. I thought you were heading out to the island, too," said Karl.

"I had just hired a boat when the other agents radioed and reported that they had recovered Ms. Stiles and found the area where she'd been captured deserted. Several men went to Kathisma, the village where the suspected kidnappers left the *Ionian Gypsy* in the hands of a hired driver, to search for them. I decided to return here in case they returned here to stir up more trouble. And sure enough, here they are." He waved a hand toward the bodies, a disgusted expression on his face.

"Good move. You gave the bastards what they deserved."

"Actually, it was—"

"What about Ms. Stiles. Was she badly hurt?"

"Man, you ask a lot of questions. She was severely dehydrated and suffering from heat trauma. She's being transported to the Lefkada Town hospital now for treatment. Boat was the quickest way to get her there."

"Have you nailed down the actual identities of the kidnappers?"

"No. I heard the gunfire and stumbled across the bodies right after you did. I haven't had time to take photographs and send them in for analysis."

"Wait, I thought you killed those men."

"No, I was trying to tell you that earlier, but you were nailing me to the wall with questions and wouldn't let me finish a sentence."

"Oh, right," Karl said sheepishly. "Then..."

Jake frowned and scratched his chin. "I have no idea who killed them."

A room door squeaked open and Jake swung his rifle toward it. "Stop, raise your hands in the air and move slowly or we'll shoot."

"No, please," Christine pleaded. "I'm not one of the blokes you're after. I'm just a hotel guest."

CHAPTER SEVENTEEN

May 25, 2016
Nikiana Hotel
Lefkada Island, Greece
1655 hours

Jamie heard Christine's voice in the hallway. The Delta had yelled for her to raise her hands in the air, she had pleaded with him not to shoot her, Karl had urged the soldier to relax, and then apparently she'd stepped out and begun talking to the men. Sitting in the room hearing only isolated bits of the conversation wasn't working. *If Christine can go out there, there's no reason I shouldn't.*

Jamie walked to the door and slowly pushed it open. "I'm coming out, too. I can't stand being in the dark about what's happening a minute longer. " Apparently, her room door hinges hadn't been oiled in recent years. They creaked loud enough that everyone stopped talking.

"Come out with your hands in the air," said a man.

"At ease, Jake, that's my girlfriend," said Karl.

She couldn't resist smiling at his possessive declaration. She raised her hands and stepped out slowly. "I'm unarmed."

She braced herself for Karl's reprimand. "I know I said I would stay in the room, but I heard all this talking out here and... It sounded safe to come out."

Instead of a frown and a furrowed brow, Karl threw her an I-know-you-too-well smile. As he continued to gaze at her, heat rushed to her cheeks. The man had a way of setting every nerve ending in her body on fire. If she warmed any more under his intense examination, she'd burst into flames.

"Come on out and join the party. The danger seems to be over for now," said Karl.

"You might want to consider finding yourself another hotel," said Jake.

Christine pointed toward one of the bodies that had been repositioned face up. "That's

Stephanos." She walked toward the other body and wrinkled her nose at the sight of it. "And this is the other one. Titos."

"I don't think they're actually Greek," said Jake with an ironic smile. "I'd wager their names are more along the lines of Ahmed and Namir."

Karl explained how the terrorists had intercepted Kallistos and Alexios when they'd returned for lunch and locked them up in a hotel room before kidnapping Baylee."

"Did you find your friend?" Christine asked.

"Yes, she's been rescued and is being transported to the hospital in Lefkada Town."

"That's a relief," said Christine.

Jamie wrinkled her brow and shook her head before turning her gaze toward Jake. "Wait a minute. I heard bits of your conversation earlier about the shoot out. Have you established who actually killed these two men?"

"No, not yet. I canvassed the building and didn't turn up any leads, so I checked into a room figuring I'd stick around for a while and make sure nothing else goes amiss."

"You came back here with some others."

"Those men headed back to Meganisi. The others are still on the boat."

Jamie shook her head. "I'm confused. If you didn't kill them and your men left the premises, who killed these men?"

*

Karl smiled; impressed that Jamie's keen mind was quickly assembling all the facts.

"We did," said a familiar voice.

"Who the hell are you people?" asked Jake in a frustrated voice. He didn't bother to raise his weapon. It appeared he'd given up on trying to keep people away from the scene.

Karl turned to see his Navy SEAL teammates Alex and Jared clad in swim trunks, carrying towels as well as weapons. "I thought you were touring Athens today."

"Drake advised us of the urgent situation so we hopped on the first available bus. We got in an hour ago. And just in time, too, it seems," said Alex.

"Yeah, lucky for you, we had your asses covered" said Jared.

Karl directed a severe look at the two men. "In your swim trunks?"

"Ye—"

"A group of us cased the entire building looking for them. How did you find them?" Jake asked.

"Once we received confirmation that Baylee had been safely extracted, we figured the worries were over. We had left our rooms and were headed for the pool when we spotted those men crouched in the hallway laying explosive lines," said Alex. "We trained our weapons on them and ordered them to raise their hands over their heads. When they grabbed their guns and fired instead, we returned the favor. And you saw who came out on top."

"That was a lucky break. It's been a long day. Hopefully this time it's really over and we can get down to enjoying the wedding," said Karl.

"Yeah, I'm ready to drink a little champagne, do a little dancing." Alex made some awkward steps across the floor and spun around, pausing to give Christine the once over and a wink.

"Maybe you should take a lesson before you go out on the dance floor and hurt yourself," said Karl.

Christine burst out laughing.

"Hey what are you laughing at?" Alex pretended to look hurt. He walked up to Christine and introduced himself. "Maybe you can drop by the reception tomorrow night. I bet you could teach me a step or two."

Christine shrugged and a pink blush crept up her neck, tingeing her already sunburned cheeks a deeper shade of red. "Sure, why not? Is it okay if my friend, Lisa comes along?"

"Of course," said Alex. "My friend here needs a dance partner. Course he also has two left feet."

"Cut it out," said Jared.

Jake shook his head, seeming unconvinced. "I wouldn't let your guard down too much yet. Where there's one terrorist, there are always more of them. I'll assemble a team to stake the place out until the wedding's over just to make sure there's no more trouble."

"I like that plan," said Karl.

"You'll have more security than they have at any Hollywood celebrity gig."

Karl laughed. "Keep it low profile so Darryl can have a normal wedding."

"Hey, what's normal any way?" asked Alex. "Do any of us even know the meaning of that word?"

"Not too much," said Karl. No normal man would banter with a bunch of people when he could be alone with a beautiful woman instead. *I'm done with the chit chat. I'll come up with a reason to go and split.*

*

Once the local police had removed the bodies and questioned every one, Karl asked for the address of the hospital in Lefkada Town where Baylee had been taken. Once the others dispersed, he turned toward Jamie. "Would you like to go visit her later on?"

Jamie beamed. "Sure, I'd like that." It thrilled her that Karl had asked her to accompany him.

"We should probably clean up first, though." He held her gaze for a moment and the silver slivers that flashed in his irises suggested he was more interested in mischief than hygiene.

Jamie shared his lack of concern with their appearance. Ripping his clothes to shreds and devouring every inch of his athletic body had much more appeal. "Oh, yes, definitely."

Karl grabbed her hand in one swift maneuver and roughly pulled her toward the room. She stumbled over chunks of drywall, struggling to match his pace. Their rush toward the room felt frenzied with attraction and heat like it had been in the early days of their relationship. She felt every bit as desperate to get him alone and naked as she had after the thwarted terrorist attack in Paris.

He pushed the door open and tugged her inside.

"Take it easy. You're going to pull my arm out of its socket," Jamie joked.

"You're a black belt, I think you can handle some jostling." His voice sounded husky with lust.

Jamie's gaze slanted toward the bed as she imagined the nature of the *jostling* to come. "Uh, yeah, maybe."

"There's so much we need to talk about, but after all the interruptions I'm thinking we might have better luck with a different method of communication." He slipped his hand free of hers and placed both of his hands on her waist.

His touch sent shivers of delight racing through her body. The surge of want that damped her panties made her gasp.

Her busy schedule had suppressed her emotions, including sexual desire. Occasionally, she'd awakened in the middle of the night, recalling the intensity of his kisses and their lovemaking. She'd curled up tighter under the comforter, ultra-aware of how cold the sheets felt against her skin, how alone she felt in his absence.

Scalding heat thawed the chill of all those long nights. Karl's virile hands—so strong, so masculine—pressed into the sensitive skin around her waist, electrifying every nerve ending.

Desire flickered in his eyes. The corners of his sumptuous lips curled up in a lusty smile the instant before his mouth descended on hers, capturing it in a fierce and possessive kiss.

His hands gripped her back, fondling her flesh as he pulled her in closer and closer until every inch of his firm body was compressed against her. A delicious shudder heated her body. His solid, masculine physique was the perfect compliment to all her curves.

She smoothed her hands over his bulging shoulder muscles before bringing them to rest on his broad back. The sculpted ridges of muscle on his shoulders, chest, abdomen and every other place on his body were hard as stone.

Like a statue of a Greek God. Apollo, Zeus, Poseidon, Hercules. Which one is he like? As his hungry kisses intensified and his hands dipped into her bra and found her nipple, lust fogged her mind. Her pulse quickened as his touch became more intimate. *He's officially the hot and sexy God.*

Grabbing the back of his head and entangling her fingers in his thick, dark hair, she pulled him in closer so she could devour every inch of his delicious mouth. A sense of urgency drove her. He reacted to her energetic kisses, tasting, licking and sucking on her lips. The air around them felt electrified by their mutual desire.

Karl's kisses acted like lighter fluid on her body. Every nerve ending blazed with hot desire. His tongue slid over her lips, prodding them apart. Her lips opened to his urging, eager for his sensual penetration. She moaned with pleasure as his tongue merged with hers in a tangle of fervent desire.

His hands skimmed over the side of her rib cage and the flare of her hip. Her heartbeat throbbed in her ears. Urgent wanting overcame her. When his strong, calloused hand reached the hem of her dress, he roughly pushed it up and skimmed his hands over the bare skin on her thighs, sliding higher, sliding closer to where she burned to have him touch her.

It felt naughty having such a sexy man fondle her in such a desperate manner despite their history together. The forbidden nature of their animal desperation further escalated her desire.

His hand skimmed beneath her panties. Jamie sighed at the sensual feel of his coarse, sinewy hands smoothing over her skin. She knew he couldn't wait to slide his hands between her legs, to soak his fingers in her wet heat.

She wanted his masculine fingers inside of her, touching, tormenting, and sending her over the edge. A rush of wet desire moistened her panties. She was ready for whatever wanton thing he wanted to do to her. No, she was desperate for it.

His breathing grew ragged as his lips dove beneath the neckline of her dress. She gasped at the sensation of his hot breath on her breast before she felt the press of his moist lips and the flick of his tongue on her nipple. His deft hands slid beneath her panties, gripping them and tugging them inch-by-inch down her legs.

Once they fell to the floor, she raised a foot and kicked them away. He was still flicking his tongue over her breasts when one of his hands slid under her thighs. His other one supported her middle back before he scooped her in one swift movement like she were a light-weight stuffed doll. He carried her to the bed and set her down gently on the mattress.

"God you're beautiful. I've fantasized about being with you again like this for so long." His gaze wandered over her body.

She lay on her back savoring the naughty vulnerability of her partial nakedness. One shoulder strap had fallen down her arm and one of her breasts was exposed. Her dress hiked up over her hips, her thighs had fallen apart, exposing her vulnerable opening to his feasting eyes. She'd never had sex half clothed before, but for some reason it was exactly what she wanted. "I want you to enter me without removing my dress."

A lewd smile spread over his face and his tongue slid over his lips. "You don't have to ask twice." After shucking off his shoes and his shirt, he began unzipping his jeans.

Jamie couldn't take her eyes off of him. Her sex pulsed with need for him as she watched his seductive striptease act. As his hand maneuvered his zipper down further, his biceps and shoulder muscles flexed and rippled. His fly open, his hands worked to pull the tight jeans and the underwear over his hips.

She licked her lips as he uncovered a slice of flesh on his lower abdomen. The wispy dark trail of hair would lead down to that part of him that delivered endless hours of hedonistic delight. He tugged the pants down lower until his cock sprung free. The muscles on the sides of his hips flexed as he hurriedly tugged them down his legs and cast them aside.

He stood over her, studying her body while his hand reached out to stroke her face. "Do you have any idea how sexy you look right now?"

"You always knew how to make me feel special," Jamie whispered.

"You are special. So special."

She watched his muscles flex and bunch, entranced as he straddled her, smoothing his hands over her shoulder and arms before they drifted down to her hips. He slid one hand underneath her buttocks elevating her hips as he slowly descended.

As his cock teased her entrance, her pussy pulsed with aching need. She wanted him to drive into her hard and deep. She arched up into him and gasped with pleasure as the crown of his penis pushed further inside.

"Don't worry, I'll give you what you want." Karl flexed his hips in toward her, pushing deeper inside.

Jamie spread her legs wider and groaned, "Oh, yes." It felt so sinful and delicious having him breach her opening, stretching and filling her.

He thrust into her, supporting most of his weight with his hands so as not to crush her as he drove in deeper.

Karl's body drove her wild. It was such a turn on watching his pumping hips, his flexing arm muscles, the beads of sweat shining slick on his chest and forehead, the muscles in his jaw tensing as wanton sensations overpowered him.

She especially liked watching his cock sliding into her. Every time it filled her so deep. *So damn deep.* Every time he slid inside of her, the pulse in her pussy intensified. She didn't want gentle, careful lovemaking she wanted him to fuck her. And fuck her hard. She arched up into him with more fury, groaning as his sweaty flanks smacked against her sensitive bud. "This feels so good."

A smile turned up one corner of his mouth, but no words escaped his lips. All his efforts were directed at seeking and delivering pleasure. And he was an expert in the pleasure delivery department.

As he increased his tempo, they became a writhing mass of limbs and sensations. The pleasure of his length sinking in and out of her hot, clenching flesh intensified.

She panted and gasped each time he slid in deep and his hips ground into her bud.

Overpowered by lusty sensation, she arched up into him, urging him deeper inside. Digging her fingertips into the hard ridges of his back, a scream of ecstasy escaped her lips as her release ripped through her.

She screamed and thrashed and called out his name while wave after wave of wanton pleasure pulsed through her body. Gripping her tighter, Karl gave in to his release, surging inside of her with one final thrust.

Karl slipped out of her and encircled her in his arms. Jamie sighed with pleasure as he held her tight, caressing her sweaty skin with his calloused fingers and gently pulling the top of her dress back over her exposed breast and shoulder. Still breathing heavily, he spoke to her in a raspy voice. "I hope that was an adequate substitute for conversation."

"Are you kidding me?" She burst out laughing, feeling high from the sex and exertion. "It was way better than talking."

"I was hoping you might say that. I think more non-verbal communication might be in order, but first I want to ask you something."

Jamie raised her head from his chest to meet his gaze. The ceiling fan spinning over their heads cooled her sweaty skin. "Sure, what?" She traced a finger over the sensual lines of his mouth.

"You asked me earlier about that last phone conversation."

"Yes," she said in a whisper, afraid that fateful night would haunt her forever.

He reached for her face, brushing the tips of his fingers over her cheek and then pushing a stray lock of sweaty hair away from her face. "All right. It might be a lot to process, but I'll tell you what I was about to say."

"Okay, Karl." He sounded so serious. Jamie's heart beat faster and she sunk her front teeth into her lower lip, anxiously waiting to hear him speak.

"When we began drifting apart, I knew letting you go wasn't what I wanted. What we once had together was too good for that. I concluded that if we spent more time together, we'd get it all back."

"I thought that, too, but it didn't seem realistic given our careers," said Jamie.

"You're right. We couldn't make it work without some kind of compromise. That's why I talked to Nathan. Got the scoop from him about his contract work with the U.S. Department of State.

"He said the pay was good, the schedule less grueling and that it still fulfilled his desire to serve his country and took the edge off his adrenaline junkie nature. I figured that could work for me, too. That night I called, I wanted to talk that over with you, see what you thought about it."

Jamie was too stunned to speak. He said all this so casually, like he was deciding whether to buy chicken or beef for dinner. *He's willing to change careers to spend more time with me?* Guilt over the unnecessary pain she'd inflicted weighed heavily on her. "Oh, Karl, I'm so sorry. I ruined everything."

"Please don't be hard on yourself. It was a misunderstanding. We weren't on the same page when it ended. But if you want to try to make it work, I'm ready to commit to you as well as to my work."

"This is really what you want?"

"Yes, Jamie, it is. At the end of next month, I plan to turn in my resignation and submit my application to the U.S. Department of State. My contract runs out then, so I have the option not to re-up. Then I'll be free to come to Paris so we can apartment hunt. We could find a place we like and live together. What do you think?"

Her heart lurched in her chest. She imagined sipping coffee over the breakfast table and strolling through Paris parks like they had in the good old days. She leaned in and planted an enthusiastic kiss on his lips. "Karl, I think that would be great. It was terrible not having you in my life. Being together is what I want."

He gathered her in his arms and pulled her in closer, massaging her back. Then an exploring hand slid under the cotton fabric of her dress, drifting over the bare skin on her back toward her buttocks and leaving a trail of hotspots behind. "I'm glad to hear that we're on the same wavelength. I want you in my life, too." His voice transformed from loving and gentle to sensual and raspy. "Now I think it's time we get back to non-verbal communication."

CHAPTER EIGHTEEN

May 25, 2016
Lefkada Island, Greece
2010 hours

The sun slowly sank toward the line of tree-covered ridges, casting a glowing orange pallor over the Ionian Sea. Once the sun disappeared behind the trees, clouds that feathered across the pale blue sky burst into brilliant shades of orange, pink and red.

Wind hummed over the water and sand, ruffling Olivia's hair and tickling her face. Baylee was safe, the threat had ended and now she and Darryl could relax and enjoy the evening together. Elated laughter escaped her lips as she strolled along the beach holding her fiancé's hand.

She couldn't stop from staring at his profile. He looked good enough to eat from every angle. His freshly shaved, chiseled face was framed by reddish-brown hair and sexy dimples accented his full lips. The ocean breeze had tossed strands of hair over his brows, obscuring the thin white scar above his right eyebrow.

In forty-eight hours, I'll be Mrs. Darryl Jennings. Darryl's last name attached to hers had such a lovely ring to it. *Olivia Jennings.* A wide smile spread over her face. The marriage license, the change to their names, the homes that would be titled in both of their names…All would be a testimony to the love they had for each other, their commitment to spend the rest of their lives together.

Darryl swung their joined hands upward. His sturdy bicep muscles flexed as he extended a finger to point out an oasis of olive trees a short distance up the beach. "That looks like a good spot for our picnic and dessert." He said the word dessert in a suggestive tone of voice.

Olivia turned toward him and grinned, knowing right away from the wicked twist of his mouth what he had in mind. *A picnic with benefits.* "Looks good to me." She wasn't sure what delicacies he'd ordered from the restaurant and packed in the whicker basket he held under his arm, but she knew her body was on the dessert menu. He planned to feast on her and she on him until they were sweaty and sated.

Privacy was theirs on this deserted beach they'd found after walking a mile or more from the hotel, making naughtiness a major temptation. Even if another couple happened to walk by when she and Darryl were entangled and naked, they'd barely be noticed in this private oasis. We might be heard, though, she thought. Control was never a factor during lovemaking. Both of them were like animals in heat whenever their bodies merged—panting, grunting, desperate.

They deviated away from the water toward the secluded spot. Darryl dropped a large towel on the pebbly ground and Olivia helped him spread it out before settling on the ground beside him and resting back on her elbows to soak up the view of their surroundings. "What a beautiful night." The brilliant colors had bled from the clouds and the sky over their heads was tinged deep purple. A full moon had risen over the ocean, casting a brilliant white path across the water.

Darryl's face glowed under the moonlight. "Lucky for me, there's a full moon so I won't miss out on any scenery I want to see tonight. Let's put first things first. Are you ready to find out what's in the basket?" One brow rose and his smile looked sensual.

As usual, the man had sex on his mind. Not that Olivia minded. She was every bit as sex-crazed as he was. Especially now, knowing they'd have two delicious weeks alone together after their wedding.

Just imagining all the crazy sex they'd have made her pussy throb with desire. Neither of them much cared for repetitious maneuvers in bed. They fucked each other senseless below waterfalls, on beaches, in parks and Olivia had even spread her legs wide in a low-lit restaurant and touched herself in front of him.

She leaned in toward him until her shoulder brushed against his arm. "Sure. Show me what you've got."

He opened the lid and pulled out a chilled bottle of wine, setting it down in front of her. He pulled a pocket flashlight from his pocket and shone the light on the label so she could read it and craned his head so he could see it as well. "Ah, this looks like a fine Greek wine. A 2013 Domain Sigalas Assyrtico. A taste of sea salt and citrus it says on the bottle. First, I'll get the lady drunk. Once I ply her with wine, cheese and such, I'll have my way with her."

"Only if I say so," Olivia teased.

"Oh, you'll go along with my plan," he said in a confident tone, a wicked smile twisting the corner of his sexy lips, making one dimple appear more pronounced than the other. "As a matter of fact, you'll spread your legs wider and beg and plead for me to fuck you harder before it's over."

God, the man turned her on. His dirty talk made her pussy contract and her nipples tighten. Her body was hard-wired for sex with Darryl. "Talk's cheap, mister Navy SEAL. Now stop talking and pour me a glass of that wine."

After turning off the flashlight and setting it aside, he pulled two glasses out from the basket. He popped the cork off the bottle, filled a glass and handed it to her.

After pouring himself some wine, Darryl turned toward her and raised his glass to make a toast. "To you, naked and begging for more."

She'd expected him to toast to the lovely evening or their impending marriage. "Oh, stop," she said with reserved irritation.

He pulled back his glass and played hurt. "What? You don't like my suggestion for a toast? I can't think of anything I'd rather toast to tonight." His eyes flashed with lust in the low light.

She knew Darryl loved her. She was a confident, secure woman. She didn't need him to gush over her, his actions were enough proof of his feelings for her, but she couldn't pass up on an opportunity to tease him and play hard to get. "That's not very romantic."

"My lady wants romance." He scratched his chin and tilted his head to one side. "Well then, let's toast to a lifetime of you and me naked."

Olivia tossed her head back and burst out laughing. "I guess that's the closest to romance I'm going to get out of you." She bumped glasses with him and took a sip. The wine tasted bitter on her lips. Even its fruity aroma turned her stomach. *2013 must have been a bad year for grapes in Greece.*

"This wine has an interesting flavor." She tried not to make a distasteful face. She'd pretend to take another sip or two and pour it out when he wasn't looking.

"Very zesty and fruity. I can see you don't like it much." Darryl's lips looked sexier than ever wet with wine.

"It's fine, really." She raised her glass to her lips again, gritting her teeth. She feigned taking a sip and quickly set it down.

"Stop the act, Liv. I can tell you hate it. Let me see what else we have here. There's bound to be something that will wash away the flavor." He pulled out a few aluminum foil-covered plates and uncovered them one by one.

"Pita with hummus and tzatziki. Black olives. Dolmathes, my personal favorite. And here's some spanikopita with big hunks of feta cheese to go along with it." He handed her a set of plastic silverware and a paper plate. "Ready to dig in?"

She salivated at the tempting spread of foods. "You bet. It all looks delicious." After digging the base of her wine glass into the pebbly ground, she leaned in to shovel some of the delicious food onto her plate.

"I love your enthusiasm," said Darryl.

She gave him a flirtatious smile before plunging her fork into a hunk of feta cheese and raising it to her mouth. The salty flavor instantly cleansed her taste buds of the wine. She craved more of the flavorful feta. In quick succession, she devoured two more hunks of it.

"Wait," said Darryl, stopping a piece of cheese traveling toward her mouth. "Let me help you with that." He plucked the square of goat cheese from the fork. "Let's ditch the silverware and eat with our hands. Let's make this a sensual dining experience," he said in a husky voice. He gently placed the piece of cheese between her lips.

She closed her lips around his finger, sucking gently and flicking her tongue over it as she moved the salty cheese around in her mouth. The salty flavor reminded her of the flavor of Darryl's semen. She longed to suck his cock until he exploded in her mouth.

He groaned as he slowly slipped his finger out of her mouth. "Oh, God, Liv, a little encouragement goes a long way with you. Not that I'm complaining."

Olivia reached for an olive. "Time for you to open up."

"I can do that."

His firm, sensual mouth had already opened by the time her hand reached his mouth. She slipped the olive between his lips, feeling a rush of lust as he mouthed her finger, sucking it in and out of his mouth. Lust jolted from her nerve endings to her breasts and between her thighs. She slid her finger back out. "I thought I better remove my finger before you choked on that olive."

"Don't worry about me, I'm doing just fine," he said. "I can see it in your eyes. You liked that. You didn't want to stop." A devilish laugh escaped his lips. "I bet images of me sucking your pussy flashed through your mind. There's nothing my tongue loves more than flicking over your clit and licking your slit until you're hot and swollen." He flicked his foot launching a small scampering lizard off into the sand.

She gasped as wet heat soaked her panties. Her pussy pulsed hot, aching for the sensual ministrations of his mouth and tongue.

"I know you want it."

Her pussy gushed again and she shifted around on the towel, trying to get comfortable. "Darryl, stop. I can't take this any more."

"Take off your skirt," he said in a commanding voice. He slipped an olive into his mouth, chewing slowly and seductively.

With trembling legs, she rose to her feet. She pulled the loose, cotton skirt over her waist, tugging it down until it pooled at her feet. She stepped out of it with one foot and the instant she raised her other one, Darryl grabbed her skirt and tossed it aside.

"Underwear, too." His hungry, predatory gaze raked over her body.

She tugged down her silk panties and kicked them away, knocking over her wine. "Oops, I got a little carried away."

"Oh, that's nothing compared to what's coming." He knelt in front of her, sliding a hand over the contours of her calf and smoothing it along the inside of her thigh. His touch left a trail of heat behind. His breath warmed her hip before he brushed his mouth over the apex of her thighs. "God, I love your beautiful, long legs. They're so sexy. I'm already imagining them wrapped around me. I'm going to fuck you so hard tonight, Liv."

Her legs trembled and her pussy ached. She was so desperate to feel Darryl's fingers inside her, his tongue skimming over her clit or his cock plunging deep inside of her. Anything would be better than this dirty talk with no action. He had to end this need that was so desperate. "Please, Darryl."

"You're so swollen and wet you can barely stand." His hot breath tickled her opening and he spoke in a lust-tinged, husky voice. "Stretch out on the towel and spread your legs. Perch on your elbows so you can watch everything I do to you, see my tongue licking your pussy. I promise to give you a good show."

Her weak legs nearly collapsed as she dropped down on the towel and stretched out her legs. "Darryl, you have to stop tormenting me like this. I can't take much more of this."

"Didn't I tell you to spread your legs?" He crawled closer, grabbing her feet and pushing her thighs apart to make room for his advancing body.

"Yes," she said in a whisper. His gorgeous mouth was just inches away from her wet aching opening. She tipped her knees out, feeling her whole body thrumming with need.

His gaze directed between her thighs and he licked his sensual lips. "Oh, now that's what I like to see. A drenched wet pussy than can't wait to be fucked." A calloused hand brushed over her clit. "Yes, that's where I'd like to taste you first."

Perched on her elbows, Olivia held her breath, anticipating that moment his mouth would connect with her flesh. His head dipped between her thighs and at first, she felt his hot breath tickling and stimulating her swollen flesh. Then the tip of his tongue flicked over her clit. She arched up into him and groaned. It felt so good. Too good. His tongue circled over her swelling nub, slowly at first and then with increasing intensity. As his tongue zeroed in on the most sensitive part of her clit, she bucked and groaned and thrashed. Intoxicating pleasure ripped through her as she climbed close to orgasm. She anticipated the plunge of a finger inside her vagina would take her over the edge.

Instead, a lubricated finger pushed into her anal opening. His invasion of her forbidden opening drove her completely insane. Once his finger was seated deep inside her, he pumped it in and out of her while his tongue flicked over her clit. "Oh, God, Darryl, yess," she screamed. She fell back on the towel as sinful pleasure exploded in her pussy and ripped like a shock wave through her body. Her hips and limbs thrashed in random directions as she screamed and shouted.

Once her orgasm subsided, she lay sprawled out on her back, her muscles spent, feeling the drug-like after effect of the sexual experience wash over her. But still, she craved more. Her gaze directed toward Darryl's shorts and the erection that tented the fabric. She was desperate for him to fuck her. But first she wanted his erection deep inside her mouth.

A sinister smile turned up the corners of Darryl's lips. "I see you enjoyed yourself. But you're staring at my cock. You want it out of my pants and between your legs now, don't you? I can tell when you're desperate for a good fucking."

She gasped as her need surged up all over again. The man knew how to talk dirty. Hot blood surged straight to her pussy, making her want him more than ever. "Yes, I want your cock," Olivia said in a breathless whisper. "I want to suck on it."

"Your sexy talk and the *I want to be fucked* look in your eyes has made me so goddamn hard I'm going to explode." He stood briefly to shuck off his clothes and then stretched out on his back, his legs spread.

Olivia pushed herself up on her hands and knees, straddling Darryl's body. Her pussy clenched at the sight of the hard lines of beautiful, toned muscle punctuated by his impressive erection. She flicked her tongue over the head of his cock, earning a wanton grunt from Darryl. She circled around the head before slowly descending over him, sucking him, wanting her mouth to feel even better to him than her tight channel.

Darryl groaned and his hips arched up toward her.

As more blood surged into his cock, she felt his size expand inside her mouth. She descended over his cock. His cock was too big to take him full into her mouth, so she supported her mouth's activities with her cupped hands.

"Fuck, Liv, I can't hold out much longer," Darryl said in a raspy voice. His head fell back on the blanket and his dimples looked deeper than ever he was so out of his mind with lust.

Wet heat gushed to her pussy. It turned her on to have so much control over him, to use her body to drive the man who belonged to her to the edge of insanity. "I want to taste you," she said, before she slid over him again, sucking him tighter than ever with the wet walls of her tongue and mouth.

"Oh, fuck, yeah." Darryl thrust up into her mouth faster and faster until he exploded and gasped in raspy breaths.

Olivia swallowed the come and strummed her finger over her lips and the rim of her mouth to collect the remainder of it. She licked it up with her tongue.

"God, that's hot," said Darryl. "I'm turned on so much, I'll be ready to fuck you in less than a minute."

"I hope so."

"Lay on your back and spread your legs. I've got something special planned for you now."

He knelt in front of her, his already rising cock bouncing against the taut muscles of his abdomen.

"What did you have in mind?"

His heavy-lidded gaze drifted toward her dripping wet opening. "I want to fuck your tightest opening. I want to feel that tight little ass of yours squeezing every inch of my cock." He gripped underneath her thighs, pushing himself in closer while he raised her legs so they fell over his shoulders.

She gasped, feeling wet and aroused over the thought of what he was about to do to her. The forbidden act they rarely indulged in.

He pushed her legs further apart and she bent her knees so he could bring himself in closer and elevate her hips. She felt the press of his cock's tip on the entrance of her anus. It felt so warm, so sensual. And so naughty to have his cock pushing it's way into this place.

She licked her lips, panting with anticipation of what was to come. She couldn't wait to feel his cock breach her anal orifice. She ground her hips up toward him.

"I love that desperate expression on your face. You can't wait to have my cock fuck your ass and my fingers plunging deep into your other hot, wet hole, can you? A double fuck is just what a naughty woman like you wants."

Olivia groaned, feeling hornier than ever from his dirty talk.

"Say what you want or I won't give it to you." His voice sounded devilish, tormenting.

She twisted with frustration and want. "Please, Darryl, don't do this to me."

"The more I make you wait, the more insane with lust you are later. And it's so damn erotic to see you want me like this. My cock is so hard for you, Liv, so goddamn hard."

The throbbing in her pussy was so intense, she placed a finger on it to assuage the agony. "Fuck me. You have to fuck me now." She stroked her pussy with more intensity and ground her hips upward to force the tip of his cock further into her anal opening.

His hips retracted and then drove into her with one long deep stroke that made her cry out from the mixed sensation of pleasure and pain. His intrusion into this forbidden place reminded her how huge Darryl's cock really was. She licked her lips as lust washed over her. "Oh, God, yes."

As she watched the sexy gyration of his hips, she gasped again when he plunged two fingers deep into her wet heat.

"You're dripping wet. And so hot," he said in a deep voice tinged with lust. He retracted his hips and drove into her again and again, matching the rhythm of his tormenting fingers.

Olivia panted and gasped like an animal in heat, desperate for the next plunge of his cock and fingers and the spread of hedonistic pleasure that it delivered. "This feels so good. So good. I want more. More."

The expression on his face drove her almost as wild as his deliberate, forceful thrusts. The way his jaw muscles flexed whenever he plunged into her, deepening his dimples, the way his emerald green eyes flashed bright with lust as his hips flexed against her body. She felt her excitement building, her inner walls starting to contract. "Oh, God, Darryl, don't stop."

She got a feral grunt in response. He appeared to be as overpowered by their coupling as she was. He continued to grind his hips into her and she gyrated to meet his tight muscled pelvis with each thrust. The wet sound of his fingers sliding in and out her and the scent of their wild fucking sent her over the edge.

She screamed and writhed and thrashed as delicious pleasure exploded in her center and then radiated with a fiery heat in every direction. The ecstasy of her first orgasm had just begun to subside when another one ripped through her. She tossed her head and screamed, feeling wickedly out of control and at Darryl's mercy.

Darryl's balls whacked against her buttocks during her throes of ecstasy and then struck her one last time as he sank deep into her anus and spewed out his release. With a wicked grin on his face, he pulled out of her and crawled across the towel to position himself beside her.

She rolled toward him so they lay beside each other, face to face. Both of them were still breathing heavily. His body glowed under the bright moonlight, every contour exaggerated by its illumination. A drop of sweat slid down the sculpted slopes of Darryl's face. She traced the path with a fingertip.

"That was amazing." His hand laced through her hair, brushing it with a loving touch away from her face.

"It was. Always is," said Olivia. The sea breeze tickled her skin, intensifying the high from all their lovemaking. She was even more moved by the cozy warmth burrowing inside her chest. "Being with you is always great," she whispered.

The desire to feel emotionally close to him was stronger than it ever had been before. Those declarations of love she could usually go without were what she craved right now. Endearing words were on the tip of her tongue, but she held back, not wanting him to feel obligated to reciprocate.

His gaze fastened on her face and his hand skimmed down her arm until it rested on her hip. "You know I'm not too big on the gushy stuff."

"Yeah, I know that," said Olivia. "You prefer body talk."

"Hell, yeah I do. We're so hot together. So damn hot," he said in a soft voice. "But I love you so much. Right now I'm looking at you and thinking how lucky I am," He smoothed his free hand over her cheek and then reached for her hand, holding it and stroking a finger over the slender diamond engagement ring she wore on her finger. "To have you in my life and be about to marry you."

His tender words filled her heart with joy. "I love you, too, Darryl."

CHAPTER NINETEEN

May 26, 2016
Nikiana Hotel
Lefkada Island, Greece
1630 hours

Mild nausea churned in Olivia's stomach. She lay stretched out on her hotel room bed with two pillows propped behind her head. She gagged as another roiling wave of unease threatened to bring her lunch up. She sat up on the bed and took several deep breaths, but the overpowering nausea intensified.

She jumped up from the bed and bolted toward the bathroom. Holding her head over the toilet, she gagged and then hurled. *Why now?* The day before her wedding was no time to be sick.

She'd traveled all over the world and rarely suffered stomach upset. Since arriving in Greece, she hadn't consumed anything sketchy. No food from street vendors, no uncooked vegetables, no water from the tap. She had devoured more feta cheese, pita bread and olives during these past three days than she'd ever eaten in her entire life, but none of those foods were a recipe for Montezuma's Revenge.

Bile surged in her throat. Even the thought of food sickened her. She gagged and hurled again.

Once the violent bout ended, she cleaned up her face and teeth. Feeling physically wilted, she sauntered back into the room and collapsed on the bed. Despite the stiff mattress, it felt amazing to stretch out on her back, to allow all her tired muscles to relax. She allowed her eyelids to flutter shut, craving sleep.

Why am I so tired? This was the first nap she'd taken in months. Her energy level was typically off the charts high even without coffee. Her jetlag wasn't any worse than the sleep deprivation she suffered on the job. On a typical workday, she often operated on four or less hours of sleep and subsisted on energy bars and motor oil variety coffee.

Whatever the cause of her nausea and fatigue, she didn't have time to pamper herself.

In less than twenty-four hours, she'd say *I do*. She and Darryl's family members and friends had traveled thousands of miles to watch them exchange vows and Olivia couldn't disappoint them. She couldn't disappoint Darryl. She loved him so much she wanted to show him her best side on their wedding day. She wanted her memories to be happy ones, not memories of running off to heave behind a bush. She'd visit a clinic, get some medicine to reduce her nausea and hopefully be better soon.

Olivia sat up in bed and released a long, frustrated sigh. She had another problem to deal with before she arranged for a check up; the dinner planned with her mother. She'd looked forward to the evening since she and her mom had always been close.

She glanced at her watch. It was already four thirty. It wouldn't take long to get to Lefkada Town, but she had no idea how busy the hospital or clinic would be. *I'll call mom and ask if it's okay to bump dinner back another hour.* Evening meals in Greece ran late anyway. Even a ten o'clock supper wasn't out of the ordinary.

After calling her mother and changing their eight o'clock reservation to nine, she dialed the front desk to arrange for transport to a recommended health clinic.

As she rushed to straighten her hair and put on a fresh outfit, an image of a chocolate gelato popped into her head. She could almost taste the chocolate, cold and sweet on her tongue. Saliva rushed into her mouth and she thought briefly about making a run to the restaurant before she left.

How can I think about food at a time like this? Not only was her stomach acting up, her mind was out of whack as well.

She pondered the possibility of pregnancy. *But I can't be.* When she'd been kidnapped in Rome and held captive on Capri Island two years earlier, Darryl's SEAL team had been deployed to rescue her.

During the ordeal, she'd taken a gunshot wound to the abdomen. The trauma had been significant enough that the attending physician in the Naples hospital had told her that she'd probably never conceive.

She'd kept the disappointing prognosis a secret from Darryl, figuring it wouldn't be necessary to tell him unless their relationship advanced to serious. After he'd proposed and she'd accepted, sharing the news had become a priority. But the night he'd proposed to her in Prague, he'd been deployed on an urgent mission and there hadn't been time to broach the subject.

While waiting anxiously for his return, she'd worked up the courage to tell him, expecting the worst. A virile man like Darryl would expect to father children. The disappointment she'd read on his face after she'd shared the news had been mingled with expressions of love and compassion. Having her in his life was what most mattered, he'd said. He had told her reassuringly that they could adopt a baby if she didn't get pregnant and their careers got to a stage where it felt right to raise a family.

The shrill ring of the phone disrupted her reverie. After answering the phone and grabbing her purse and a plastic bag in case another nausea bout struck, Olivia rushed from the room to catch her ride.

"Miss looks very sick," the driver said as he opened the car door and waited for her to slide across the seat.

She shrugged, determined not to make anything of it. Faking wellness might be necessary tomorrow if she didn't make a rapid recovery. "I just ate something that upset my stomach. It's nothing serious."

But the more she thought about it, the more she suspected her condition wasn't food-related. Her CIA partner, Steve Cahill, had often teased her saying she had an iron stomach.

He'd shaken his head when she stopped to buy a soft round of bread filled with mystery meat and vegetables from a street vendor in Afghanistan and washed it down with a can of soda. "How do you know there aren't roasted rats inside that thing?" he would say.

Steve often popped digestive enzymes or antacids after meals to settle his stomach while she suffered no ill effects after nearly every dining experience.

As the driver maneuvered the car around another nauseating hairpin curve, he spoke to her again. "Americans get sick very often here." His dark eyes, partially obscured by unruly dark curls, were visible in the rear view mirror. Olivia pulled the plastic bag from her purse, feeling another uncomfortable surge in her stomach. "That's comforting news."

"No, really. You just need a day or two to get used to the water."

She opted to agree with the man. He meant well. "I'm sure you're right." She glanced out the window, noticing the variety of boats moored in the harbor. Lefkada Town was a busy place compared to the sparsely populated town where the hotel was situated.

As the car passed rows and rows of boats, her nausea gradually subsided. She breathed out a relieved sigh. It would be embarrassing to throw up in the car. All at once, a craving for pretzels assaulted her. She could taste the salt on her tongue and imagined the satisfaction she'd feel crunching her teeth into them.

What is with this food obsession? She'd almost be willing to tackle an innocent bystander to get her hands on a single pretzel. She recalled the glass of cold beer she'd downed the last time she'd eaten pretzels and potato chips in a sports bar. Imagining the smell of alcohol sent bile climbing up her throat. She held the plastic bag to her face and vomited.

Framed photos of various Greek islands decorated the hospital waiting room walls. Grandmothers, parents and children of all ages occupied every chair in the small, square room. Some of the adults bounced infants in their laps. Olivia didn't see a single person wearing touristy clothes, didn't hear anyone speaking any other language except Greek.

So much for that Americans always get sick theory. Where are they, then? After checking in and filling out the requested forms, she sat in a chair that had become vacant after another patient was called back.

As the minutes ticked by, exhaustion washed over her and she sunk lower and lower into the hard plastic chair. Her eyelids felt painfully heavy, but the coughing, sneezing, moans of discomfort and the occasional shrill call of a patient's name kept her from drifting into slumber. After more than an hour, a woman stepped into the lobby and called for Olivia.

Her muscles felt heavy and tired and she collapsed into a chair in the room where the nurse led her and waited. Minutes later, a man wearing a white coat and a stethoscope around his neck stepped into the room and introduced himself as Dr. Papopoulis. "It should be easy to remember because the way you say it rhymes with Acropolis," he said with a smile after he introduced himself.

Olivia forced a smile and when he asked her what had brought her to the clinic, she described her symptoms. He flipped through the papers she had filled out earlier, frowning before looking over his spectacles at her. "How long has your stomach been upset?"

"Just today. I felt fine until this morning." She recalled how the wine she and Darryl had shared on the beach had turned her stomach. She appended a description of that incident to her story.

"Do the symptoms usually occur right after a meal?"

"No, not really." When he asked what she'd recently eaten, Olivia gave him a laundry list of recent meal and snack items.

When he asked if she'd had diarrhea and she said no, he looked even more perplexed. "Could you be pregnant?"

Olivia felt a flicker of hope. *Is it possible? The doctor in Naples said I probably couldn't conceive, but he didn't say it was for certain.* "I'm not sure. I've been living with my fiancé. Actually, we're getting married tomorrow."

Dr. Papopoulis grinned and spoke in a proud, patriotic voice. "It's wonderful that you're getting married here in Greece. What a good choice you have made. There is no place more romantic than the Greek islands. Even though I have lived here my whole life, I still never get tired of looking at that water."

"It really is beautiful. The sea is so blue. I've been here three days already and feel like I don't ever want to leave. My mom is loving it here, too. She's talking about renting an apartment here next summer." She let out a long sigh. "Our wedding would be so perfect if I could just pull myself together."

"Don't worry. It can still be perfect once we figure out what's going on. Are you currently using birth control?"

"No, but I suffered a gunshot wound to the abdomen a few years ago. They said I might not conceive because of the damage."

"Hmm. That sounds serious."

He asked more questions about the nature of her injuries and she did her best to answer each one thoroughly.

"I'm going to order a pregnancy test first. If that test comes back negative, we'll take it from there. If you are pregnant, I'll give you a list of foods that will settle your stomach so you'll be able to relax and enjoy your wedding."

She appreciated the doctor's patience and thorough attention to her situation. "Thank you, Dr. Papopoulis."

He held out a plastic cup and instructed her on how to prepare the sample for the urine test.

As she slipped from the room and walked toward the restroom, she was lost in thought. She still couldn't wrap her brain around the possibility. A baby. Her and Darryl's baby.

Oh, my God. She knew there would be complications to this sudden change in their relationship, but at the same time, the possibility thrilled her. She willed herself not to let excitement overwhelm her. More than likely, she'd leave the clinic with a negative pregnancy test result and a bottle of pills.

She returned the vial to the physician and sat in the room, trying to distract herself during the wait. Frenzied thoughts incited even more worry. *How would Darryl react? Would a baby mean an end to my career? Would I even want to work? Would I be a good mother?* She'd never cared for a baby before. *I wouldn't have the first idea how to change a diaper or to breastfeed.* She'd never thought much about having children until she'd met Darryl.

Maybe mom would stay with me for a week after the baby is born. She could teach me whatever I need to know. She told herself to stop letting her thoughts run away. *You're setting yourself up for disappointment.*

She glanced up at the clock. Five minutes. Ten minutes. Why is this taking so long?

Dr. Papopoulis rushed back into the room looking harried and out of breath. "I apologize for the delay. An emergency came up with another patient."

"I understand." She paused. "Am I pregnant?"

His dark brown eyes looked at her over the rims of his glasses, showing genuine compassion. "I'm so sorry, Miss Simpson. But the test came back negative."

CHAPTER TWENTY

May 26, 2016
Lefkada Town Hospital
Lefkada Island, Greece
1750 hours

Olivia sighed and dropped her gaze to the floor, trying not to let disappointment weigh her down. *Damn. Why did I allow myself to believe it was possible?* She'd studied the sonograms showing the extent of the damage. The perforations in her uterus and one fallopian tube had been repaired, but the surgeon had warned her that the residual scar tissue would likely impair conception.

Dr. Papopoulis cleared his throat. "I know you're disappointed, but try to look ahead to tomorrow's wedding. You're going to marry the man who loves you and that's what matters most. It appears you've picked up some sort of bacterial infection. I'm going to write you a prescription for anti-nausea medication and antibiotics. There's a pharmacy across the street where you can buy these items. I'm sure you'll feel much better soon."

"I appreciate that." She feigned a smile. *It's better that I'm not pregnant. A sudden baby would complicate things before we even have a chance to adjust to married life.*

A nurse stepped into the room and spoke to the doctor in a hushed voice.

"Please excuse me, an urgent matter has come up."

She shrugged. "No problem. I'll wait." She glanced at her watch. Six thirty. Realizing she still had plenty of time before the dinner with her mother, she made a mental checklist of what she'd do next. She'd ask a receptionist for Baylee's room number, drop by to visit her and then fill her prescription before heading back to the hotel.

Dr. Papopoulis stepped back into the room. "I am very sorry to trouble you further, Miss Simpson, but there seems to have been an error with the urine samples. We'll need to do another test."

Olivia gasped.

Olivia deposited the new urine sample at the nurse's station and strode briskly down the hall toward her patient room wondering how long the wait would be this time. Even five minutes would seem like a day. She struggled to silence that insane hope that was already jumping up and down and celebrating, and debating about whether the baby was a boy or a girl.

"Olivia, is that you?"

She swung around when she heard Darryl's voice. *Shit. What is he doing here? I'll act casual and keep quiet about the urine test unless it turns out positive.* "Darryl, hi. I wasn't expecting to see you here. Did you come to check on Baylee?"

"Yep, I just came from her room. She's doing great. They've been hydrating her through an IV. She's alert and feisty as ever and if she continues to make progress, they'll release her early tomorrow morning. But what are you doing here, Liv? Why didn't you mention you were sick?"

Olivia shrugged. Appearing nonchalant around the man who knew her best wouldn't be easy. Nervous sweat dripped between her breasts and her palms felt clammy. "I didn't want to worry you, that's all. It's nothing serious. My stomach's been a little upset so I came to get a prescription for antibiotics. I'm glad to hear Baylee's doing so well."

"Me, too. But now I'm worried about you," he said in a gentle, soothing voice. He leaned in closer and his brilliant green eyes studied her face. "You look so pale. If I'd known you were sick, I would have come here with you." He reached for her, cupping her face in his hands.

"It's okay, really. I was trying not to interfere with tradition. You know, about us not seeing each other the day before the wedding." She grinned.

Darryl shook his head, concern still radiating in the depth of his green eyes. "That's the least of our worries. We don't have to leak a word about this to our mothers. Let's focus on getting you well. What room are you in?"

She pointed to an open door nearby. Her heart lurched. Dr. Papopoulis would step in any minute and tell her a second time that the pregnancy test was negative. Hearing the disappointing news would be even harder to take in front of Darryl. And if by some miracle the doctor proclaimed a positive result, he might faint dead away at her feet.

When they entered the room, Olivia was surprised to see the doctor was already waiting. He glanced up from the chart he held in front of him and grinned. "Is this the lucky man?"

She cleared her throat and forced a smile. "Yes, Dr. Papopoulis, this is my fiancé, Darryl Jennings." There was no hiding the unsteady tremor in her voice.

"I'm doctor Papopoulis." The doctor extended his hand to greet Darryl. "I'm delighted to say I have some excellent news for both of you."

A deep furrow appeared on Darryl's brow and he took a step back and adopted an intimidating, shoulders retracted stance. "Excellent news. What do you mean?" His voice sounded stern and protective. "My fiancé looks very pale and she says she's been vomiting."

Dr. Papopoulis didn't appear to be the least bit intimidated by Darryl's protectiveness. He gave him a condescending smile. "She looks completely normal considering her condition."

Olivia drew in a sudden breath and without thinking said, "Oh, my God."

"Her condition?" He turned toward Olivia. "Liv, what is this all about?"

Tears brimmed in her eyes. "I think he's trying to tell us we're going to have a baby."

CHAPTER TWENTY-ONE

May 26, 2016
Lefkada Town Hospital
Lefkada Island, Greece
1805 hours

Darryl felt like he'd arrived late to a movie and was trying to catch up with the plot. Except this was no movie. This was his life playing out in front of his eyes. First he'd been surprised to find Liv at the hospital sick and now she and the doctor were ranting on about a baby. *A baby.* But Liv couldn't be pregnant. The surgeons in Italy had said there wouldn't be any babies. *So what the hell is this baby talk about?*

He cleared his throat, determined to approach the confusing situation with a cool head. "Did you say baby?"

Dr. Papopoulis's broad smile revealed a row of straight sturdy teeth. "Yes, Mr. Jennings, that's exactly what she said. After she described her symptoms to me, I ordered a pregnancy test and her test came out positive."

Darryl was still too stunned to speak.

Creases appeared on the doctor's forehead. "That expression on your face suggests this wasn't a planned pregnancy. Olivia mentioned her hospital stay in Italy and that you thought you might never be parents."

Planned pregnancy? Parents? Holy hell. "It is a bit of a surprise," Darryl stammered, knowing his poorly articulated phrase was the biggest understatement of the year.

When Olivia had said she couldn't get pregnant, he'd been devastated at first. He hadn't given even a passing thought to letting her go, though. She was the woman he wanted.

Their unconventional careers weren't all that compatible with raising kids anyway, he'd told himself whenever nagging images of fatherhood crept into his mind.

Months had passed and he'd gradually resigned himself to the fact that he and Olivia would always be a childless couple unless they adopted. *And now this.*

Dr. Papopoulis scratched at his chin and shifted more of his weight onto one foot. "Um. I see."

Damn it, what's wrong with me? Darryl knew Olivia and the doctor expected him to burst with delight after this sudden announcement, but his excitement warred with fear over how they would handle a pregnancy and raising a child.

Responsible parents didn't turn their child over to a nanny for weeks or months while engaging in life-threatening work. *That wouldn't be right. Our child deserves more than absentee parents.*

Their relationship might change. It had been so perfect lately, with the exception of the time they had to spend apart. If Liv were pregnant, would she be too exhausted for sex? Would her lack of desire worsen after the baby's birth?

It would take some getting used to if his high-energy Liv transformed to a lethargic and moody stranger. *You asked her to marry her. That means you tell the woman you love how happy you are and pretend you're happy until you find a manly way to cope with this sudden surprise.*

"Darryl, why aren't you saying anything?" Olivia said in a loud, unsteady voice.

Darryl blinked and gazed up, feeling a lurch of pain in his chest when he saw the expression on Olivia's face. Her big, dark eyes overflowed with tears, her smooth skin looked deathly pale and her lips trembled. "Oh, Liv, I'm sorry. This news was a bit of a shock. I'm just trying to process it, that's all." He felt annoyed with himself. Why had he blurted out that instead of saying something positive like he'd intended?

"I think I liked your silence better." Olivia whirled around and walked with a huffy stride from the room.

"Hmm…" mumbled Dr. Papopoulis with a frown.

Darryl strode out the door, calling out to Olivia's retreating back, "Hey, wait. I didn't mean to say it like that."

Olivia didn't respond. If anything, she appeared to be walking even faster. As he chased her down the hallway, he reminded himself that mending her feelings mattered the most.

He was in love with her. Many details would need to be worked out, but not today. During their two-week honeymoon, they could talk about all the logistics and figure out the best way to make it work. It would bring them even closer making those plans together.

He'd always wanted a family. He loved kids. His niece and nephew had kindled his desire to become a father. He could picture himself practicing ball with his young son in the back yard or teaching him how to ride a bicycle.

He tried to block out all the difficulties his children would face. Life in 2016 differed greatly to Darryl's childhood years. No one had ever been shot dead between classes when he was in high school or received death threats on social media. Now the threat of terror was everywhere with so many new insurgent groups popping up and recruiting followers. Most of them were active in developed countries, including the United States.

People like us have babies, he told himself. He and Olivia's children would make today's troubled world a better place. He thought of all he'd accomplished since enlisting with DEVGRU.

Without the efforts of his SEAL team, many hostages wouldn't have been rescued; many terrorists would still be at large to attack again. Important dignitaries, diplomats and everyday civilians would have perished had the dedicated Navy SEALs not stopped perpetrators planning dark missions.

Although he didn't know the details of her work, he knew Olivia was constantly fighting for justice. "Please stop, Olivia. We have to talk." Only steps behind her now, he reached for her arm, but she jerked away from his grasp.

"I don't want to talk to you now," she said in a huffy voice and then fled from him.

Darryl realized he'd bruised her badly. On top of his blunder after the news, her hormones had to be raging. He shuffled after her. "Please don't do this to yourself. It might hurt the baby."

She swung around to face him, her voice shaking with anger. "Now you're worried about that?"

"Of course. I wouldn't want any harm to come..." He took a deep breath before speaking. "To our baby."

Her brown eyes flashed with anger, standing out in stark contrast with her sheet white face. She might appear weakened by her condition, but it sure wasn't evident in her demeanor. "You can barely say it, Darryl. Spitting out those words was a major strain for you, wasn't it? Y—"

"I'm trying to be honest with you, Liv. I'm excited, but it was a shock to even see you at the hospital and then I walk into the room to learn you're pregnant."

Olivia was silent.

Darryl forced himself to continue. He owed it to her to push his shock into the background and reassure her. "We love each other and I'm going to spend the rest of my life with you. And now I'm going to become a father, too. Liv, this is what I always wanted, but I tried to let go of that because us being together was what mattered to me most. Now we'll have it all. Each other. And our child. Please, let's go back and talk to the doctor and then I'll get you back to the hotel so you can rest."

A wan smile swept over Olivia's face. "Can you imagine what our mothers would say if they were here?"

Darryl took a step toward her and reached for her hand. She clasped it and held on. "I'm guessing they'd say our wedding was doomed since we saw each other the night before the wedding. But I can't even imagine what they'd say about the pregnancy part. My mom probably thinks I'm still a virgin."

Olivia burst out laughing and a touch of warm color tinged her cheeks. "Not my mom. She knows me better."

"Yeah, and I bet you talk. Women always do. But don't tell me. I want to be able to look her in the eye after tonight." Darryl squeezed her hand. "Are you ready to go back and talk to the doc?"

"Not yet." She dove into his arms, holding onto him like she never wanted to let go.

CHAPTER TWENTY-TWO

May 26, 2016
Lefkada Island, Greece
1850 hours

Silence reigned during the trip back to the hotel. Olivia couldn't think of a word to say. She gazed out the window, wishing she felt as relaxed as the vacationers she saw outside. On the side of the street away from the harbor, carefree tourists browsed in shops, holding up T-shirts and colorful beach wraps. A man stood on the corner, drinking an open beer from a bottle.

The gravity of her pregnancy struck her. She would soon be a mother and she had to do everything right. She could keep working for a few more months, but toward the end of her term, it wouldn't be realistic for her to be in the field anymore. She'd be slow, clumsy and uncoordinated and probably groggy and dim-witted. Those changes could put her life, the life of her baby, and the life of her long-time CIA partner, Steve, in jeopardy. He deserved much better than a hormone-crazed female functioning at half capacity. That would be no good. No good at all.

Darryl gently bumped his shoulder against hers. "Liv, stop worrying."

She blinked, snapping out of her trance and directing her gaze in his direction. "I'm just thinking. Like you said earlier, this is a lot to process. Now that the excitement has died down, I'm feeling overwhelmed."

Darryl reached for one of her hands and squeezed it. "You're fidgeting all over the place. Tell me what's going on in that brain of yours."

"So many things. How a baby is going to affect my career for one." She launched into her concerns about Steve's safety and how it would be jeopardized if she couldn't perform up to her normal standards.

"Liv, you might surprise yourself. You're strong and up to anything. That's not likely to change much during pregnancy. Of course I don't like the idea of you placing yourself in danger ever, especially now. But you have to do what's best for you. I'm going to be your husband, but I don't want my worries to influence your career decisions."

"What about after the baby's born? Both of us are gone all the time."

"I'll support whatever you want to do. I could take a few months leave of absence until we find a suitable nanny who can care for our child in our home."

"You want to hire a nanny to raise our child?"

"No, not really. But a lot of working parents make that choice. Maybe one of our moms would be willing to help out. My mom is crazy about babies. I went into this marriage knowing you had a career so I don't expect you to quit. If you want to take a leave of absence or stay home with the kids, I'll support that, too. I need to finish my twenty years of service so I can collect retirement and then I'll look for work that keeps me home more."

Olivia was moved by his thoughtful answers. "To tell you the truth, I've been feeling burned out at work lately anyway and was thinking a career change might suit me. Would it bother you if I resigned and stayed at home until I finish conjuring up a Plan B?" She wondered if Darryl would lose respect for her. He'd always known her as the independent career woman. *She's the me I'm used to, too.* What if she ended up bored out of her mind changing diapers and preparing bottles? She was used to the excitement, adventure and travel associated with her fast-paced career.

He wrapped an arm around her shoulder and pulled her in closer and kissed her gently on the cheek. "Of course not, Liv. If you want to stay at home with the kids, that would make me very happy. And if you decide later that you want a career, I'll support that, too. Let's just take it one day at a time and do whatever feels right."

His acceptance of her idea thrilled her. Her mind raced ahead with other plans, ones she'd considered after she'd fallen in love with Darryl and the dream of having a family had surfaced. She'd stuffed those ideas into the recesses of her mind after she'd been shot. "The thought of being a mother thrills me. I could stay at home with the kids and work."

"How would you do that?"

"I was thinking about launching a consulting company. I could recruit and hire retired military personnel and special operations agents for multi-operational security and intelligence companies doing covert missions overseas."

"That sounds like an interesting idea. I never heard you mention it before."

"I wanted to research the idea thoroughly first. Everything I found indicated that work could be lucrative, but I saw no urgent reason to make the jump this soon until now."

"It will still be grueling."

"I'm sure. I'll need to communicate with people at all hours of the day and night and conduct interviews and detailed background checks, but at least the work will be challenging. By doing interviews virtually, I'll be able to work at home. I can always hire support staff and a person to help me around the house so I can spend more time with the kids."

Darryl acknowledged her words with an approving nod. "You're a genius, Liv. You've got all sorts of great ideas up your sleeve. Did you say kids? As in more than one?" He nudged her with his shoulder and grinned.

She released a light-hearted laugh. Talking her plans over with Darryl made their situation seem exciting rather than daunting. "I'm getting a little carried away aren't I? But if it happened once, maybe it can happen again."

"Maybe you're right. Tell me more about this work burn out you've been experiencing. You've said a few things recently that made me wonder if you needed a break. But I want to hear more."

Olivia met his gaze and held it. "After we said goodbye in Italy, I missed you so much. I started to get really irritated with all the government red tape, and work began to feel like a chore."

"Why didn't you mention anything?"

"I don't know. Everything in life has its highs and lows. I thought maybe I'd get back the fire again eventually, but it never happened. This last stint away felt like an eternity. I couldn't wait for it to end.

"I got sent to one too many dusty, godforsaken places in Afghanistan and Iraq I suppose. And even though Steve's a great partner, there's a lot of backstabbing and favorite playing in the organization. Some of the least competent operatives run off in a crisis while others that stick out the worst situations are blamed for others' errors.

"I get sick of all the bullshit after a while. I know for sure being a CIA operative isn't what I want to do the rest of my life. When I start my own company, I'll find highly qualified, dedicated people who can really shake things up in a desperate situation. And now with a baby on the way...I've got other things to think about than just my career."

"You'll be a great mother, Liv. And you'll be great as a company executive. You can do anything you put your mind to."

"I appreciate your confidence in me, Darryl. That means a lot."

He pulled her in close and nuzzled her neck. "I mean every word. I'm lucky to have you in my life and our wedding day is going to be even more exciting now that we have a baby on the way."

"I'm so happy, Darryl. Being pregnant still feels like a miracle."

He placed his hand on her stomach and gently stroked circles over it. "It is a miracle. Our son or daughter is growing inside your beautiful body."

She felt the tender warmth of his touch even through the silk fabric of her blouse. Soon her flat stomach would protrude as their child's arms and legs grew larger and his or her features became more pronounced. A smile turned up the corner of her lips when she imagined the boy or girl gazing at her with emerald green eyes like Darryl's.

CHAPTER TWENTY-THREE

May 27, 2016
Lefkada Island, Greece
0900 hours

"If I hadn't put up a fuss, I'd still be in that hospital," Baylee whined. She strode on the beach with Nathan, relishing the fresh air. The rising sun basked the fir and olive trees on the hills in golden light. Fluffy clouds, painted shades of brilliant orange by the morning sunlight, hovered over the hills. The sea, not yet fully illuminated by the sun, was a deep midnight blue. Only a light breeze blew that morning, making the water look like a dark sheet of glass. *Ah, freedom.*

After being kidnapped by the terrorists, she'd felt like a prisoner a second time at that hospital. It had been five in the morning when she'd finally been released. The first thing she'd wanted to do upon release was walk for miles on the beach. The hospital staff didn't need to know that she had no intention of following their recommendation of three more days of bed rest.

"Not even a kidnapping and severe dehydration can cramp your style."

"I know I was obstinate. But that place made me stir crazy. That IV drip rehydrated me enough after one night, I could have left yesterday. But no, they insisted on keeping me. So I stayed another night. But when the doctor started talking about extending my stay further, my patience flew."

"Fortunate for you, the man's an insomniac and does rounds in the middle of the night. And what do you mean it flew? You were impatient from the get—"

"I would have gone nuts if I'd had to lay around in that bed any longer. And I didn't fly all the way to Greece to miss Darryl and Olivia's wedding." A dolphin leaped from the smooth calm water just a couple hundred feet from shore.

When another one jumped, Nathan pointed toward the ocean. "Wow, did you see that? There must be a pod of dolphins out there."

"You're changing the subject. You think I acted like a bitch, don't you?"

"Of course not. You know I have no patience with fake niceties. If you hadn't fussed and argued until you got your way, I would have feared you'd had brain damage."

"Thanks for that." Making a fist, she gave him a playful swat in the shoulder.

"As for me, I like your feisty obstinate ways. And now that I've got you alone here on this beach, there's something I want to ask you."

"Okay, but first you'll have to catch me." Giggling like a young girl, she skipped away from him and then broke into a run, sprinting toward the sea. She kept running even after her legs struck the water, splashing water and slowing her progress. She dove under the water and then surfaced, smoothing her wet hair from her eyes. The cool, refreshing water snapped her out of the lethargy she'd felt in the hospital. She laughed, feeling elated and alive. Seawater dripped from her lashes.

Pushing off the stony bottom, she swam a head-raised freestyle, occasionally glancing over her shoulder to see how much of a lead she had over Nathan. The beach had ended and slopes of white limestone jutted out over the water. She heard a loud splash close behind her. Nathan's strokes were long and powerful. She had to act fast—he was catching up with her.

She saw the lust in his eyes. Knowing what he'd do to her when he caught her made her heart race with excitement.

She looked down to see layered limestone undulating on the shallow bottom below. She allowed her feet to touch down. She shuffled across the uneven bottom in the waist deep water, ducking underneath a branch of a fragrant fir tree that hung over the water.

*

He stopped swimming and watched as she ducked underwater to reach for something. *Another sea urchin, perhaps?* She had collected several of them over the course of their visit. Seconds later, her head broke the surface of the water. In her hands, she held her bright orange bikini top and bottoms.

Holy shit. Blood raced to Nathan's cock. There was only one logical way for this game to end.

"Perfect morning for a skinny dip." She draped the scanty swimsuit over one of the branches.

His heart beat faster. He strode toward her with a new mission in mind. To fuck her senseless right here in the sea. "You know better than to tempt me like this."

"Do I?" She strode into shallower water where her smooth abdomen and her breasts, slick with water, were clearly visible. She stood facing him, sliding her tongue across her lips as she began massaging her fingers over her nipples.

Nathan swam toward her, his head raised so he wouldn't miss a second of this delicious show. "I'm going to have to teach you a lesson." He dropped his feet to the rocky bottom just in front of her, feasting his eyes on her full, sensual breasts. *God, I want one of those in my mouth this instant.*

"I hope your lesson involves sex," she said in husky, seductive voice. "Because I'm desperate to be fucked. I almost died yesterday and now I want to celebrate being alive by indulging all of my senses. The water feels so good tickling my clit, pushing inside my hole. The sea breeze on my wet skin makes me feel almost high. But none of that comes close to the rush I'm going to get when you drive your cock deep inside me."

Nathan's cock stiffened to the point of pain. After freeing his erection from his swimsuit and draping it carefully over a branch next to Baylee's, he grabbed her roughly around the waist. "Wrap your legs around me and I'll give you what you want. I'm hard and ready."

In an instant her slender white thighs wrapped around him, her heels dug into his back and her slit brushed against his cock. Gripping his erection with one hand and holding her tight around the waist with the other, he positioned himself just outside her opening. He placed his other hand around her back, clenched his jaw and drove in deep. The sensation of her tight walls squeezing him stole every coherent thought from his mind. Grunting like a primitive being, he thrust into her again. Baylee responded to his deep penetration with a series of lusty, out-of-breath pants and gasps.

"Oh, God, Nathan, yes. Fuck me, fuck me," she cried.

Water splashed and surged as he continued to thrust inside her. Even in the ocean, her walls were slick and hot and so damn tight he felt like he would die from the primal pleasure gripping his cock. Cupping the back of her head with one hand, he pulled her face in closer and claimed a kiss.

It wasn't gentle, though. It was lusty and demanding and full of heat. He drove his tongue through her parted lips and swept it across her teeth. Her tongue met his and tangled. It was so erotic the mating of their tongues and writhing bodies surrounded by a world of blue water.

"Oh, Nathan, I'm going to come," Baylee whimpered.

He thrust in harder, faster as a crazed delirium overcame him. The instant she came he knew he was going to blow. Their fucking was so crazy and uninhibited he grappled to retain control. "Come, baby. You've got to come."

He felt the rhythmic clenching of her walls before she screamed and thrashed with ecstasy. Her beautiful, rounded breasts bounced each time he pounded into her and her face and neck were flushed from exertion. The erotic show was too much for him and he exploded inside her after her orgasm faded.

"Fuck, that was amazing," said Nathan. Their coupling had drained every ounce of manhood from his cock, but he knew his body would produce plenty more in time for their next interlude, which with any luck would happen in a few minutes.

"Yeah, it was," Baylee said in an out-of-breath voice. She leaned in and laid her head on his chest. "Now as I recall, there was something you wanted to ask me?"

Laughter tumbled from Nathan's lips. He felt elated from the sex and the salty ocean and holding his sensual ball of fire so close like this in his arms. After carefully freeing his swimsuit from the tree branch, he reached into one of the pockets.

The conventional down-on-his-knees proposal that he'd been worried he'd make of a mess of wouldn't work. A marriage proposal while they stood facing each other, waist deep in the sea and breathing heavily after fucking each other senseless on the other hand..."Yes, I do have something I'd like to ask you." He reached for her hand and held it up just above the water. "I love you when you're a grump at the hospital and I love you when you mouth off to me and when you're a wild sex maniac. Every day is better with you around. Anyway, the hell with this bull shit. I've never been too good with speeches anyway. Will you marry me, Baylee?"

She gasped and jumped up and down in the water before leaping into his arms. "Hell, yeah, I'll marry you."

Nathan pulled his hand from the water to show her the ring he'd picked out for her.

"Nathan, that's beautiful."

"No, you're beautiful." He gripped her slender finger and gently slid on the engagement ring.

EPILOGUE

May 27, 2016
Lefkada Island, Greece
1630 hours

Darryl and Olivia stood angled in toward each other on a platform overlooking the Ionian Sea. The brilliant blue water redefined the color cerulean. Lingering clouds from an earlier rain hung over the sea and the nearby islands along with a brilliant rainbow. The splash of waves on the sand and the call of gulls flying overhead served as a wedding march.

Olivia's such a beautiful bride. Her dark eyes sparkled with joy. Her fair skin had tanned to a golden brown after a few days on the island. A minister stood between them reading citations from the Bible.

Jamie looked at Karl and smiled. He looked so handsome wearing his Navy uniform. The blue uniform fit snugly around his strong, bulky shoulder muscles and broad chest. Its color exaggerated the flecks of green and silver in his ocean blue eyes. He reached for her hand and held it, pulling their clasped hands into his lap. The sturdy grip of his strong calloused hand made her feel so safe, so content.

After visiting Baylee at the hospital, Karl had patiently waited for Jamie to compose an article about the kidnapping and rescue and submit it to France 24. The two dead men had been identified and the man who had delivered the message to Nathan had been taken into custody.

Karl agreed that her message mattered. The world needed to know that the Muslim Alliance was one step closer to being crippled. She'd consulted with the Special Operations team and Officer Laskaris to make sure she wasn't releasing any information they didn't want printed including the compromised identities of the SEALs.

Once Jamie hit the *submit* button on her email program, clothes had been discarded and she and Karl had spent all night making love.

The next morning, they'd joined the group of swimmers for an adventure. The *Ionian Gypsy* had taken them out to Skorpidi Island. They'd swum the channel to the private island of Skorpios, stroking their way around its perimeter, while armed Russian bodyguards watched from the shore to make sure they weren't up to mischief. Swimming beside Karl in the clear blue sea and turning to breathe and seeing bodyguards and a mansion surrounded by stone walls, she'd felt like she was starring in a James Bond movie. She'd enjoyed the company of the swimmers so much she'd ended up exchanging emails with Lisa, Christine and a famous romance author named Jayden that she'd met on the boat.

After lunching with the swimmers in Nidri, she and Karl had returned to the hotel and spent all afternoon lounging in the sand by the sea and talking while waves lapped at their feet. They'd exchanged more stories about their pasts than ever before.

She'd learned many new things about Karl...He'd played soccer as a youth, while most of the other boys his age had gone for football or baseball. He'd been penned a nerd in elementary school because his favorite hobby was conducting science experiments in the basement with various chemicals.

He'd once ended up in the principal's office for two hours in sixth grade after he'd caused an explosion in science class after mixing up a particularly volatile concoction. She'd known already that he was fiercely loyal, that he loved deeply, that he believed in committing one hundred percent to any task he took on.

It's wonderful to love a man I admire and who understands me. Not to mention one who's gorgeous and an Adonis between the sheets. Just thinking about the uninhibited lovemaking they'd indulged in the past two nights sent erotic tingles racing up her spine.

Jamie glanced around, observing the crowd of people gathered to celebrate the couple's special day. Family and friends of the bride and groom dabbed their eyes with tissues as the pair exchanged hand-written vows and declared their love and commitment to each other.

All of the SEALs Jamie had met in Paris were in attendance. Christine and Lisa sat beside each other in the last row of seats, having received last minute invites from the couple.

The bride and the groom stood barefoot. Their naked feet combined with their formal attire added a tinge of *sexy* to the wedding. *Perfect for a pair with a reputation for being a bundle of heat together.* Darryl looked handsomer than ever in his dress uniform.

The silver SEAL trident he wore on his lapel shone brilliant under the afternoon sun. The ivory, silk dress that clung to Olivia's fit body showed off her tan and was decorated with tiny beads and stitching that trimmed the scalloped neckline and ankle-length hem.

When Jamie turned toward Karl and held his gaze, he mouthed *I love you*. Jamie squeezed his hand and silently spoke those same words in return, wanting to declare her love for him while Olivia and Darryl spoke their vows.

Once the rings were exchanged, the minister gave Darryl permission to kiss his bride. He accepted the suggestion with robust enthusiasm and as their lips collided, claps and whoops erupted from the audience. Both had wide smiles on their faces as they reluctantly released each other from the embrace, exited the stage and walked down the aisle as Mr. and Mrs. Darryl Jennings.

Jamie imagined herself as the bride. Walking down that aisle beside Karl, knowing that he was her husband. *One day our friends and family will watch us vow to love each other forever like this.* For a moment, she wondered whether they'd marry on a beach or in her hometown and then realized it didn't matter.

Even if they married in a tattered marriage chapel in Las Vegas, the day would be wonderful because they'd be together. The nerve endings in her cheeks tingled at the thought of this future she knew belonged to her. One of love and passion and companionship.

As if Karl read her mind, he turned toward her and kissed her cheek.

"That was a beautiful wedding, wasn't it?" she said. She found it hard to verbally express what being a part of the couple's once-in-a-lifetime day had meant to her. The setting had been idyllic, the weather perfect, but the love expressed between Darryl and Olivia had made the deepest impression on her.

"Yes, it was." Deep emotion was evident in the depths of his blue eyes.

Jamie sensed he had more to say so she studied his face, waiting for him to express his thoughts.

"When we get married, I think we should make it easier for our families and have our wedding in the States."

A smile spread over Jamie's face. She was so excited she couldn't think of what to say. "Oh, wow."

"I also have an idea for our honeymoon." He gave her a seductive wink.

"Oh, and what's that?"

"I think we should spend two weeks on a romantic Greek island. Lefkada, perhaps. We'll do a little swimming, a little lounging on the beach and make love the rest of the time. Oh, and of course we'll feast on delicious Greek food. What do you think about that?"

Jamie laughed and leaned in and kissed Karl's cheek. "I think that's an excellent plan."

THE END

ABOUT THE AUTHOR

Sabrina Devonshire, an avid swimmer most of her life, can usually be found near or immersed in a body of water. If she's not seeking an endorphin rush in a pool, lake or ocean, she's often encouraging people to work out or writing a romantic suspense or magazine article.

She received a John Woods Scholarship and an Arizona Commission of the Arts Professional Development Grant toward her participation in a 2007 Prague Summer Program Writing Workshop. She also studied writing in Arizona and northern California and has a M.S. degree from the University of Arizona.

Sabrina loves traveling to off-the-beaten-path places where phones and electronic devices tend not to work well. Peru and Belize are two of her favorites. Sabrina lives in southern Arizona with her husband, two children, and fluffy dog, Sugar.

To read blog posts, blurbs, excerpts and more, check out the Sabrina Devonshire Exotic Romantic Adventures web site at www.sabrinadevonshireromances.com

Made in the USA
Charleston, SC
11 January 2016